The Case of the Artful Crime

Nancy opened the front door of the restaurant and saw that the rainstorm was in full fury, spattering the front lot with its driving torrents. Closing the door, she turned back toward the kitchen. A clap of thunder exploded overhead, followed by a flash of jagged lightning in the windows.

In that split second of brightness, Nancy spotted a dark figure in the dining room.

Nancy flattened herself against the hallway wall. Her heart was hammering in her ears as she wondered if the intruder had heard her. She hoped that the thunder and rain had masked the sound of her footsteps.

Moving soundlessly, Nancy made her way to the entrance of the dining room and peered at the intruder. What was going on?

With one startlingly swift gesture, the figure raised his arm. Nancy saw the glimmer of the knife in his hand as it swung over his head—then slashed through the painting's canvas!

Nancy Drew
Mystery Stories

Available from MINSTREL Books

NANCY DREW MYSTERY STORIES®

THE CASE OF THE ARTFUL CRIME

CAROLYN KEENE

PUBLISHED BY POCKET BOOKS

New York   London   Toronto   Sydney   Tokyo   Singapore

A MINSTREL PAPERBACK *ORIGINAL*

 A Minstrel Book published by
POCKET BOOKS, a division of Simon & Schuster Inc.
1230 Avenue of the Americas, New York, NY 10020

Copyright © 1992 by Simon & Schuster Inc.
Front cover illustration by Aleta Jenks
Produced by Mega-Books of New York, Inc.

ISBN: 0-671-73052-5

First Minstrel Books printing April 1992

10 9 8 7 6 5 4 3 2 1

Printed in the U.S.A.

Contents

THE CASE OF THE ARTFUL CRIME

1

A Birthday Surprise

"Surprise!" Nancy Drew sang out as she turned her blue sports car into the restaurant parking lot.

Carson Drew smiled. He'd realized his eighteen-year-old daughter was up to something. Now he had an idea what it was. "This doesn't look like the law library to me," he teased.

Nancy pulled into a spot right outside the low, white, stucco building. The ceramic tile around the door and windows gave the restaurant an air of Southwestern elegance. An arched sign over the front door read The Arizona House.

"Did you really think I would drag you to the law library on your lunch hour?" Nancy asked skeptically.

"At first I did," her father said with a laugh. "I know how you get when you're on a case. You don't think about anything else."

1

Nancy had to admit her father was right. Once she was immersed in solving a mystery, there wasn't much that could distract her.

But, as it happened, right now she wasn't working on a case at all. She'd made the whole thing up, telling her father she needed his help in finding her way around the law library of nearby Westmoor University so she could research a clue. It had simply been a ruse to get him away from his busy law practice for a special lunch.

"I wouldn't forget your birthday," Nancy said with a toss of her shoulder-length, reddish-blond hair.

Carson Drew shook his head. "If you want to know the truth, I was so busy preparing a defense for court tomorrow that *I* forgot it was my birthday."

"Like father, like daughter, I guess," Nancy said brightly as they got out of the car and headed up the fieldstone walkway. "Bess says this restaurant is terrific," she added, referring to her close friend Bess Marvin. "She's been working in the coatroom, filling in for a friend who's out sick. Bess just raves about the food."

Carson held open the restaurant door for Nancy. "If Bess says the food is good, then I believe it," he commented. "I've never seen anyone who loves food more than Bess."

Stepping inside, Nancy and her father became part of a small crowd milling in the wide front hallway. Off to the left was a lounge. To the right was a coatroom, which could be seen from the hallway. Nancy checked to see if Bess was there, but the room was empty. "The dining room looks pretty busy," Carson noted. "I hope they can seat us."

"No problem, Dad," Nancy assured him. "We have a reservation." Weaving through the crowd, Nancy made her way to the reservation stand and greeted the maître d'. "Hi, I'm Nancy Drew. We have a reservation for one o'clock."

The slight, dark-haired young man adjusted his glasses and ran his finger down the list of names penciled into the reservation book under Tuesday. "Drew . . . Drew . . . Drew . . ." he muttered.

"It must be there," Nancy insisted, frowning. "I called last week."

"I'm sure you did," he said. "But I'm afraid that someone has completely botched up the reservations." He gestured to the people waiting in the hallway. "Most of them had reservations, too. I'm sorry, but you'll just have to wait."

"All right," Nancy said, turning away in frustration. How could this be happening? She'd wanted everything to be perfect.

As Nancy headed back to her father, she saw that Bess had already found him. "Isn't this place fabulous!" Bess gushed when she spotted Nancy. "I was just in the kitchen getting myself some lunch. They're so nice about feeding their employees. You can have whatever you want, except the shrimp and lobster. They're too expensive. I was telling your dad that even though the place is busy, I don't have anything to do. It's such a warm day, no one has coats. It *is* unusually warm for early May, don't you——"

Noticing Nancy's expression, Bess stopped her chatter. "What's wrong?" she asked.

"They've lost our reservation," Nancy told her friend glumly.

"Oh, no!" Bess cried. "I'd heard something about a whole bunch of reservations being messed up. Everything is going wrong around here lately. Let me go talk to Lee. He's the maître d'. There's *got* to be a table for you." Brushing her blond hair back off her shoulders, Bess made her way to the reservation stand.

Despite her annoyance, Nancy had to smile as she watched her friend in action. First Bess tried charm, batting her bright blue eyes at the maître d' and smiling her prettiest. Then Bess's hands flew to her hips and storm clouds of anger swept across her face. All the while, Lee kept shaking his head or shrugging his shoulders helplessly. Things didn't look too good.

Nancy was just about to suggest a different restaurant to her father when Bess waved them forward. "They're setting up a table for you now," she said.

"Follow me," Lee said, leading them into the bustling main dining room.

"It's beautiful, isn't it?" Bess said as she and Nancy followed Carson and Lee to their table.

Nancy nodded, taking in the creamy pastel pink

4

walls with a border of native American art along the very top. A cactus garden in the center of the room was lit by an overhead skylight.

Lovely though the restaurant was, something about it seemed wrong to Nancy. Then she realized that it was the unframed oil paintings that hung on the wall to her right. They were landscapes, but the scenes seemed to be of the northeast. There were tall pine trees, snowcapped mountains, and sparkling blue lakes. There's nothing Southwestern about them at all, Nancy thought. What an odd choice. Then she dismissed the paintings from her mind.

Turning her attention back to Bess, Nancy asked, "So how did you get us a table?"

Bess lowered her voice so that the maître d' wouldn't hear. "I reminded Lee that Shawn wanted to see you."

"Shawn?" Nancy questioned.

With a sheepish look, Bess explained, "Shawn Morgan. He's the owner and chef. I hope you don't mind, but Shawn has this problem, and I told him all about you."

"Bess!" Nancy cried, then lowered her voice. "Don't you remember? I told you I didn't want to take any more cases for a while. I'm planning to visit Ned before he starts exams." Ned Nickerson, Nancy's boyfriend, was away at Emerson College. Nancy had been so busy throughout the early spring that she'd planned—and then had to cancel —five different trips to see Ned. "I haven't seen

5

him for ages." There was a pleading look in Nancy's blue eyes.

"Don't worry. This is just an itsy-little simple thing that you can probably figure out in a day," Bess cajoled. "You've just got to talk to Shawn. He's a great guy, and I promised him you would help. Please, Nancy."

"Here's your table," Lee said. The staff had hastily set up a small table near the swinging kitchen door.

"Is this the best you can do?" Bess asked the maître d'. "This is Siberia." She turned to Nancy. "That's restaurant talk for the worst table in the house."

"It's fine, Bess," Carson said with a quick glance at his watch. "I only have an hour until I meet with a client."

Nancy and her father took their seats, and Bess pulled up a chair beside them. "Don't you have to work?" Nancy asked with a laugh.

Bess checked quickly over her shoulder. "I don't see any customers with coats, and I hate just sitting there. It's boring. I'll go back in a minute."

A waiter appeared dressed in black pants, a black denim apron, and a blue denim shirt. A red bandanna at his neck put the finishing touch on his western attire. Nancy looked around and saw that the other waiters and waitresses were dressed the same.

"Welcome to the Arizona House," their waiter said as he handed Nancy and her father menus.

"Try the mesquite-grilled salmon," Bess advised,

reading over Nancy's shoulder. "It's Shawn's specialty. He's an awesome cook. Chef, I mean. Chefs don't like to be called cooks."

Nancy was still studying the menu when Bess suddenly grabbed her arm. "I don't believe it!" she exclaimed. "There he is. That's him!"

"Who?" Carson asked.

Bess leaned in close to Nancy and her father. "See the guy who just came in?" she whispered. "The one standing in the hallway? That's got to be Harold Brackett. You know who I mean—the food critic who reviews restaurants for *The Illinois News* and *Fine Foods* magazine."

Nancy followed Bess's gaze across the restaurant and spotted a handsome man of medium build in his early thirties. He was wearing an expensive-looking gray suit and a yellow silk tie. His clothing and regal manner gave him a distinguished look. "What makes you think that's him?" Nancy asked.

"Everyone around here is talking about Harold Brackett's review of Le St. Tropez in yesterday's *Illinois News,*" Bess said. Le St. Tropez was the poshest restaurant in River Heights.

"Elliot, the prep cook, has a friend who works there," Bess continued. "He says no one even suspected it was Brackett until the end of the meal. But then this guy who had been sitting all alone started telling the waiter everything he hadn't liked. Brackett gave the restaurant a pretty poor rating. In the review he griped about all the same things that the complaining guy at the restaurant

7

had talked about. The guy must have been Harold Brackett."

"Harold Brackett hates every restaurant he reviews," Carson noted, putting down his menu.

"I know. That's what everyone says," Bess said. "So anyway, since he reviewed Le St. Tropez, that means he's in this area. And this is the city's newest restaurant. Don't you think he would check it out while he's here?"

"Sounds logical," Nancy said. "But why are you so sure that's Harold Brackett? Have you seen a picture of him somewhere?"

Bess shook her head. "Oh, no, no one has. Harold Brackett likes to remain anonymous. But Elliot's friend said he was tall, had very dark hair, and wore a yellow tie. Rumor has it that Brackett *always* wears a yellow tie. Plus, he's alone. And a gorgeous guy like that could easily get a date. It has to be him."

"Maybe he's on a business trip," Carson suggested.

"Or maybe he's a creep and nobody likes him," Nancy teased.

"He's definitely not a creep," Bess said, frowning. "You can just tell from looking at him. He looks like a soap opera star. Or at least a game show host." Bess got up and looked toward the kitchen. "I want to warn Shawn that Harold Brackett might be here. I'll be right back." A moment later, Bess disappeared into the kitchen.

Nancy and her father had just finished ordering

when Bess returned to the dining room. Behind her was a sandy-haired man in his mid-twenties wearing chef whites. Grabbing the chef's arm, Bess nodded toward the man with the yellow tie. "That's him," Nancy overheard her say.

"Could be," Shawn said slowly, scrutinizing the man who was following Lee to a table near the doorway. "He looks like the type. I'll make him an extra-special lunch, just in case."

Bess turned toward Nancy's table and said, "Shawn Morgan, this is Nancy Drew and her father, Carson Drew. Nancy is the friend I told you about. The one who might be able to help you."

Shawn smiled ruefully as he shook their hands. "Pleased to meet you both. Has Bess told you about my problem?"

"No," Nancy replied. "Just that there is one."

"I'd better get back to the coatroom," Bess said. "I just saw a mink stole walk in. Can you imagine? In this weather? Have a good lunch."

As Bess crossed the restaurant, Shawn settled into the chair she'd been sitting in. "I'll make this story short so you can enjoy your lunch in peace. Here's the bottom line. I think someone is trying to put me out of business. Every time I turn around, something is going wrong."

"What sort of problems have you been having?" Nancy asked.

Shawn shrugged. "Take your reservations, for example. Bess told me what happened. I truly apologize, but that's just the kind of thing that's been going on. This morning I discovered that someone had torn off the bottom half of all the pages in the reservation book. I'm pretty sure the book was fine when I left last night. And I was the last person out. We copied the names on the top part into a new book, but the names and numbers on the bottom couldn't be found."

"That's terrible," Nancy said.

Shawn shook his head wearily. "Yesterday it was the exhaust system in the kitchen. Grease and cooking smoke were backing up into the dining room. The repair guy found cloth napkins jammed into the fan. The day before that, someone messed around with the plumbing in the bathrooms. All of the toilets were backed up. If this keeps up, I'm out of business."

"Do you suspect anyone?" Nancy asked.

"Not really," Shawn answered with a sigh.

"Who, besides you, has keys?" Nancy questioned.

"No one," Shawn replied. "Though about a week ago, I couldn't find them for a few hours. Finally, I spotted them on the floor in the hallway. I figured I'd dropped them."

"But someone could have made copies in that time," Carson suggested.

"It's possible, I suppose," Shawn said. He pushed back on his chair and folded his arms. "I've sunk every penny I have into this place. The remodeling alone has put me in debt over my head. If I can't make a go of it, I'm in big trouble. Nancy,

Bess says you're the best. Do you think you can help me?"

Nancy twirled the stem of her water glass between her fingers as she thought. This didn't seem like a difficult case. She was fairly certain that someone on Shawn's staff was responsible. It had to be someone who could move around freely without seeming out of place. With a little luck, she would pinpoint the culprit and still have time to head off for a visit with Ned. Besides, Shawn seemed like a nice guy. She hated to see his business ruined.

"I'll give it a shot," Nancy said. "And I have an idea. Why don't we pretend that you're hiring me as a new waitress? That way, I can snoop around the restaurant without anyone suspecting."

"That's great," Shawn said, standing. "Could you start tonight?"

"No problem," Nancy agreed. "What time?"

"Five o'clock would be best. Wear black pants and comfortable shoes. I'll supply the rest of your outfit. Nancy, I can't thank you enough," Shawn said, looking relieved.

"I'll do my best," Nancy promised.

Shawn glanced across the room at the man Bess had insisted was Harold Brackett. A tall, willowy waitress with long red curls was just leaving the man's table.

"Looks like Loreen got his order," Shawn said. "I'd better get back into the kitchen and make sure his food is perfect." Shawn excused himself just as Nancy and her father's meals arrived.

11

"Wow! This salmon is great," Nancy said, sampling her lunch. "How is your burrito?"

"Delicious," Carson replied. "I'm glad we can spend this time together now, since I won't be seeing much of you for a while."

"Sure you will," Nancy said, smiling. "This case won't take long."

"The last time you said that, you were on the case for weeks," he reminded her.

Nancy laughed. "I remember. But that case looked a lot simpler than it was. This one is pretty straightforward."

"Famous last words," Carson said with a chuckle. For the next twenty minutes, Nancy and her father ate their lunch and chatted happily. With both of them so involved in their work, they often dashed past one another in the hallway of their home, exchanging just a quick hug and brief words. Nancy was glad they had this time to talk.

Glancing across the restaurant, Nancy noticed that the man with the yellow tie was about to taste his lunch. "Dad, do you think that guy really is Harold—" Nancy cut herself off the minute she saw the expression on the man's face. Something was wrong—very wrong. His eyes watered, and a crimson flush swept up over his cheeks.

Clutching his throat with one hand, the man grabbed the edge of the table with the other and pulled himself to his feet. His eyes streamed with tears. He opened his mouth to speak, but was unable to utter a sound.

2

Trapped!

Nancy and her father leaped up from their seats. "Dad, I think he's choking!" Nancy cried.

In seconds the two of them were across the room. A low murmur spread through the restaurant as all eyes turned toward the gasping, red-faced man.

A petite woman who had been dining at a nearby table rushed to the man's side. "I'm Dr. Hordell," she told him. "Where is the pain?"

The man collapsed into a chair, his forehead drenched with sweat. A waiter rushed over with a glass of water, which the man gulped. When he was done, he pointed at the fish on his plate.

"That!" he gasped. "The fish!"

Picking up the man's plate, Nancy examined the heavily herbed fillet served on a bed of yellow rice. Gingerly, she sniffed it. Almost instantly, her sinuses tingled and she jerked her head away.

"See what I mean?" said the man, starting to regain his voice and composure.

"May I have that, please?" Shawn requested, coming up beside Nancy.

"There's some very powerful spice in that fish," Nancy warned, handing him the plate.

As Shawn sniffed, a frown creased his brow. He took a clean fork and flipped the fish over. "How on earth?" he muttered. Under the fillet was a layer of bright green paste.

"I don't even keep this stuff in my kitchen," he said. "It's *wasabi*. It's used exclusively in Japanese cooking, and I don't offer any Japanese dishes at the Arizona House. Someone must have snuck the *wasabi* in and added it after I prepared the fish."

"But it *is* edible," Nancy said.

"Yes, but it's so hot that most people eat just the tiniest dab at a time. This poor gentleman got a mouthful when he ate his fish."

"I'm sure it was extremely unpleasant," Dr. Hordell said. She turned to the man. "Keep sipping water. Eventually the burning will pass."

"Unpleasant! It was much more than unpleasant!" the red-faced man boomed, mopping his brow with a linen napkin. His enunciation reminded Nancy of an actor's perfect speech.

"*Wasabi* is powerful stuff," Shawn agreed. "I can't tell you how sorry I am, sir."

Just then, Bess rushed over. "What happened? Oh, Mr. Brackett, are you okay?"

14

The man's eyes darted back and forth. "What did you call me?"

Bess blushed. "Sorry. I know you want to keep your true identity a secret. But I know you're Harold Brackett. The food here is really the greatest. It's just that lately everything is going wrong. We think someone is deliberately trying to mess things up for the restaurant. You can't believe what this person is doing—wrecking the plumbing, tearing the reservation book. I'll bet that same person did this to your food and—"

"Bess," Nancy warned. She didn't think Shawn wanted this bad news made public.

"Oh, um . . ." Bess stammered. "I just wanted Mr. Brackett to understand why—" Suddenly a glimmer of doubt flashed in her eyes. "You *are* Harold Brackett, aren't you?"

The man shrugged. "I suppose, since you found me out, there's no sense denying it."

Bess looked at Nancy triumphantly.

Carson cleared his throat. "If no one needs me, I'll return to my lunch," he excused himself.

"So will I," said the doctor. "Just keep drinking cold fluids and you should be fine," she added as she returned to her table.

"Mr. Brackett, I am deeply sorry about this," Shawn apologized once again. "You can't imagine how sorry. Please give us a second chance—on the house. I promise you this terrible prank won't be repeated. I'll serve your meal personally."

15

The crimson flush was fading from Brackett's olive complexion. "I suppose I might," he agreed, taking a sip of water. "Let's just say I like to give new businesses the benefit of the doubt. This is a charming place you have here. Who did your decor?"

"I did," Shawn told him proudly. "With help from Loreen, our head waitress. She's the one who served you."

Brackett grimaced. "Yes. I believe that was the name tag worn by the woman who delivered the fish of death."

Nancy noticed the red-headed waitress serving another table. For a moment Loreen looked back toward Harold Brackett's table curiously, then returned quickly to her work.

Loreen, thought Nancy, registering her first possible suspect. Could Loreen be the one sabotaging the restaurant? She had handled the fish after Shawn had prepared it. But what could be her motive?

Looking at her watch, Nancy realized that her father's lunch hour was nearly over. She excused herself and rejoined him at the table. "Sorry, Dad," she said as she took her seat. "I thought this would be a nice quiet lunch."

"I don't know, Nancy," her father said good-naturedly. "You're like a magnet for excitement. If you don't find it, then it finds you."

"At least you can't say my life is boring," Nancy answered with a laugh.

16

"No, I would never say that," Carson agreed wryly. "Shawn seems to be a nice enough guy," he went on. "I hope he can make a go of this place. The last owner couldn't seem to make it work."

"What last owner?" Nancy asked. "Have you been here before?"

Her father nodded. "Many years ago. At that time, it was a popular French restaurant called Chez Jacques. The food and service declined for some reason, unfortunately. Then Le St. Tropez opened, and everyone began eating there instead." He glanced around the dining room. "I didn't realize that this building was still here. I wonder when it changed hands."

"That's something I should find out from Shawn," Nancy said, taking a quick peek under her fish for any signs of *wasabi*.

After dropping her father back at his office, Nancy spent the rest of the afternoon thinking about the case. Whoever the culprit was, he or she was fairly bold. Spreading the hot *wasabi* on that fish had to have been done quickly and in a moment when no one was looking.

At the moment, Loreen was the most likely suspect. She'd had the opportunity. But did she have a motive? Nancy decided to find out more about Loreen that evening.

By five o'clock Nancy was driving back to the Arizona House in her blue Mustang. She wore a pair of tapered black pants, as Shawn had requested, and a deep blue T-shirt.

17

The Arizona House was on the outskirts of River Heights in an extremely wealthy area. In this part of town, mansions were set far back from the winding country roads. The restaurant itself was at the end of a narrow, wooded road.

Once again Nancy pulled into the lot and went in the front door. This time the restaurant had an entirely different atmosphere. It was cool and quiet. The only sound was the clinking of glass and silverware as the tables were set for dinner in the empty dining room.

"Nancy!" Shawn greeted her, stepping out from the lounge. "I was just getting these things from the storeroom for you." He handed her three cellophane bags. In them were the fringed denim shirt, the bandanna, and the apron worn by the Arizona House waiters. "You can put these on in the ladies room downstairs," he said, directing Nancy to a set of narrow steps to the right of the coatroom.

She had just finished dressing when Loreen walked into the large, well-lit room. Surprise filled the redhead's face. Her expression quickly changed to a look of unmistakable irritation. "Who hired *you?*" she asked.

"Shawn did. This afternoon," Nancy replied.

"Why wasn't I informed?" The waitress frowned.

"I really don't know," Nancy said as sweetly as she could manage.

Loreen's green eyes narrowed as she gave Nancy the once-over. "Weren't you here at lunch today?" she asked.

18

"Yes," Nancy said, nodding. "I mentioned that I was looking for a job, and Shawn hired me on the spot. Wasn't that nice of him?"

"Real nice," Loreen replied sarcastically. "That Shawn is one super-duper guy. I think I'll go talk to Mr. Wonderful about you right now," she added as she slammed the door.

Nancy was about to follow her when she bumped into Bess. "What did you say to her?" Bess asked. "She was breathing fire."

"She's not too happy I was hired," Nancy replied.

"I guess not. She usually hires and fires the waiting staff," Bess said with a shrug. "Loreen's sort of the manager around here."

"I'd better go upstairs and see what's happening," Nancy said, slipping through the door. At the top of the stairs, Nancy looked around for Loreen, but the head waitress was gone.

"Okay, Nancy," Shawn said, looking up from the reservation book. "Ready for the grand tour?"

"Did you talk to Loreen?" Nancy asked.

"Don't worry about her," Shawn said. "Sometimes she forgets who's the boss around here. I told her that I'd decided to train an extra waitress in case we need help serving the upcoming summer crowd. Everybody on the staff wants some time off over the next few months."

"Did that explanation cool her down?" Nancy asked.

"She went off in a huff," Shawn said, "but she'll get over it."

"Why didn't you tell her the truth?" Nancy asked.

An uncomfortable look came over Shawn's face. "The fewer people who know why you're here, the better," he said.

Nancy had to agree with that. "Do you think Loreen could be the one causing the trouble?" she pressed.

"I don't want to think so," Shawn said. "But I suppose anything is possible."

"Does she have a reason to wish you harm?"

"No," Shawn said decisively. "Absolutely not."

Nancy followed Shawn through the restaurant as he introduced her to the waiting staff and the busboys and girls. In the lounge, they ran into Roy, the bartender. Nancy smiled as she was introduced to the older man with the pleasant expression, receding hairline, and pot belly.

Now that the restaurant was calmer, Nancy had time to look it over carefully. As she trailed Shawn across the dining room, her attention again was drawn to the oil paintings on the wall. "How did you select these paintings?" she asked Shawn, still thinking that the artwork seemed strangely out of place.

"I bought them from a friend," Shawn answered shortly.

Just then, Bess joined Nancy and Shawn. "How's it going?" she asked.

"Fine," Nancy replied. "I've seen everything but the kitchen."

"Bess, why don't you show Nancy the kitchen area?" Shawn suggested. "I have a million things to do right now."

"No problem," Bess said. "Come on, Nancy."

Bess led Nancy through a set of swinging doors into a large, spotless, industrial kitchen. "This is the only part of the restaurant that hasn't been redone," Bess confided. "It's your basic restaurant kitchen."

Bess opened a drawer full of forks, knives, and spoons. "Here's the silverware, if you need it." She then pulled open the white doors of a freestanding wooden cabinet near the front kitchen door. "All the linens are in here. Napkins, tablecloths, aprons, that kind of stuff. The busboys and girls usually deal with all that, though."

Next, Nancy followed Bess to the middle of the kitchen. At the largest of three steel counters, a short, silver-haired man stood furiously pounding a ball of dough. "I'm about to introduce you to the world's grouchiest human," Bess whispered. "Prepare yourself."

Nancy grinned. "Go for it."

"Jack," Bess called, her voice especially genial. "Meet Nancy. She's a new waitress. This is chef Jack Henri."

Jack looked up quickly. For a moment, Nancy felt as though his piercing dark eyes were boring right into her. Then he grunted and returned to his work.

"He's not exactly Mr. Personality," Bess whispered. "He makes great desserts, though."

21

At another counter stood a skinny, bespectacled young man of about twenty who was busy feeding carrot sticks into a food processor. Bess paused beside him. "This is Elliot Mifflin," she said. "He's a prep cook. Elliot, meet Nancy."

"Hi," Elliot said.

"Hi," Nancy replied. "I see you've got that down to a science," she added, nodding toward the slivered carrots.

"That's me, Mr. Slice and Dice," he said with a nervous laugh.

"Elliot!" Jack called gruffly, his rough voice bearing the trace of a French accent. "Get me maraschino cherries from the bar."

Immediately, the food processor stopped whirring. "Right away. Oh, I should have done that earlier," Elliot mumbled as he wiped his hands on his apron and hurried out of the kitchen.

"Doesn't he remind you of the white rabbit in *Alice in Wonderland?*" Nancy whispered as they moved away toward the back of the kitchen.

Bess's hand flew to her mouth, stifling her laughter. "He does," she said, giggling.

At the back of the kitchen, near the rear entrance, was a small alcove. On the wall hung a metal case with card-filled slots. "These are the time cards," Bess told Nancy. "Shawn will make up a card for you. You punch this time clock when you come in for each shift and punch out when you leave. And you're supposed to use the back door. The front entrance is for customers only."

22

Nancy was only half-listening. She'd suddenly become aware of a faint, disturbing odor in the air. "Bess, do you smell smoke?" she asked.

"This *is* a kitchen," Bess teased. But her expression turned serious as she sniffed the air. "You're right. That doesn't smell good at all."

"Jack!" Nancy called as the girls dashed out of the alcove. "Jack!"

There was no reply.

"Oh, no!" Bess shouted when they came to a halt in the middle of the kitchen. The tall linen closet had toppled onto its side—and it was a roaring blaze of flame!

Immediately, Nancy reached for the red fire extinguisher on the wall. She took aim and squeezed the handle, but nothing came out. "This thing is empty," she cried, tossing it aside. "Let's get out of here!" Since the overturned cabinet completely blocked the door to the dining room, Nancy grabbed Bess's arm and pulled her toward the rear exit.

Bess ran ahead, lunging for the back door. She grabbed the handle and tugged, but the door wouldn't budge. "Nancy!" she cried, panic filling her voice. "I can't open it!"

Nancy yanked at the door handle. "It's locked."

"Oh, no!" Bess wailed. "We're trapped!"

3

Hotter by the Minute

Anxiously, Nancy glanced at the ceiling. "The sprinkler system should be on by now," she observed.

"Well, it's not," said Bess woefully.

Looking back over her shoulder, Nancy saw that a six-foot-high wall of fire now stood between them and the dining room. It was spreading rapidly, the flames leaping over to a stack of boxes on a cart. Black smoke began to fill the room.

"Help!" Bess cried, then covered her mouth as the smoke choked her suddenly, causing a coughing fit.

Thinking fast, Nancy ran to one of the large industrial sinks. She turned on the cold water, grabbed the hand-held sprayer, and aimed it at the fire. But the spray wasn't strong enough to subdue the flames.

Throwing down the sprayer, Nancy splashed herself with water. "Come on, Bess. Get wet." As Bess joined her, still coughing, Nancy found two cloth napkins and soaked them. "Hold this over your mouth and nose," she gasped, handing Bess a napkin. "And get down on the floor, below most of the smoke."

As Nancy and Bess crouched, Nancy's eyes swept the kitchen, looking for another way out. She spotted two long, rectangular windows near the ceiling. They would be hard to reach. But maybe she could throw something up to break the glass. That would give her and Bess more air, but it might also fan the flames.

Suddenly Nancy no longer needed to make that decision. The kitchen door swung open with a bang. Shawn was in the lead, followed by Lee, the maître d', and one of the waitresses. Each of them aimed a fire extinguisher at the wall of fire.

When the flames blocking the door died down, Shawn kicked aside the charred, collapsed cabinet. While the waitress and Lee continued spraying the flames, Shawn ran to Nancy and Bess. Bess grabbed his arm, then doubled over in another coughing fit.

"We need to get you two out of here fast," he told the girls.

Nancy took two steps forward, but then staggered to the side. Her head spun, and a queasiness was gathering in the pit of her stomach.

"Sit," Shawn directed, helping Nancy to the

25

floor. "I'll be right back." He swept the still-coughing Bess from the kitchen. A moment later, he returned for Nancy.

Nancy felt Shawn's strong arm around her shoulder. "The smoke gets you before the flames do," he explained, guiding her out of the kitchen.

As Shawn led her into the dining room, Nancy noticed that a handful of employees had gathered outside the door. She recognized the head waitress, Loreen, and the bartender, Roy, in the group.

"The fire department is on its way," Loreen reported to Shawn. Her green eyes flashed on Nancy, who was still leaning heavily on Shawn's shoulder.

"I see it took you all of a half hour to get into trouble," Loreen jeered as Nancy collapsed into a chair beside Bess.

"Knock it off, Loreen," Shawn snapped. "Why don't you go out to the parking lot and wait for the fire trucks? We'll need to direct them to the kitchen."

Loreen glared at him before she headed off.

"I'd better see how they're doing in there," Shawn said as he turned back toward the kitchen. A brunette waitress, who introduced herself as Anne Marie, offered Bess and Nancy water and cool cloths.

"What happened?" came Jack's gruff, French-accented voice. He was walking into the dining room from the front hall. Elliot was right behind him.

"There was a fire in the kitchen," Nancy told him wearily.

"Oh, my goodness!" Elliot fretted. "I hope I didn't leave a burner on or something."

"No," Bess said, wiping black soot from her cheeks. "It was the linen cabinet."

"Do you or Jack smoke?" Nancy asked Elliot. "The fire could have been started by a stray cigarette."

Jack looked insulted. "There is no smoking permitted in my kitchen," he replied.

My kitchen, Nancy noted, wondering about his possessive attitude. "Where did you go?" she asked him. "We thought you were still in the kitchen."

The dessert chef arched his eyebrows disdainfully. "Not that it is any of your affair, but I went to see what was taking Elliot so long."

"There were no cherries at the bar, so I had to go downstairs to the storeroom," Elliot explained. "I couldn't find them, so Jack had to come down and help me look." Sheepishly, he held up a jar of bright red cherries. "I found them."

Nancy smiled, then shifted her attention back to the fire. "Is anything else stored in that closet, any kinds of chemical solvent that might have ignited like that?"

"I don't believe so," Elliot replied.

"Absolutely not," Jack said.

Slowly, Nancy pulled herself up from the chair. Sirens sounded in the distance. The fire department should be able to figure out what happened, Nancy

27

told herself as she walked back toward the kitchen. She stood in the doorway and observed the damage. The kitchen floor was awash with a sudsy foam, the walls were charred, and smoke hung in the air like an evil dark cloud. Alone in the middle of the kitchen stood Shawn, holding a linen napkin over his nose and mouth. He walked over to the stove and flicked on the exhaust fans to clear the smoke, then surveyed the area with an expression of complete despair.

He sensed Nancy's eyes on him and looked up. "I should never have called the fire department," he said as the sirens grew louder. "Now I'm going to get zonked with fines on top of everything else."

"Because your kitchen extinguishers were empty?" Nancy asked.

"And my sprinkler system failed," he added.

"Why did those things go wrong?" Nancy asked.

Shawn climbed up onto a counter and reached toward a valve in the ceiling. "I can tell you why the sprinkler didn't work," he offered as he turned the valve. "It's been shut off." Climbing back down, he picked up the empty extinguisher that Nancy had thrown to the floor. "This was a brand-new extinguisher," he said. "It's never been used. Someone must have deliberately emptied it."

"What you're saying is, this was arson," Nancy surmised.

"It sure looks that way," Shawn agreed grimly. "I never lock that back door, except at night. Food is delivered through that door all day long, and the delivery people walk right in. Somebody got hold of my keys and locked that door from the outside."

The scream of fire engines told Nancy that the firefighters had arrived. Moments later they hurried into the kitchen.

"Nancy," Shawn said. "Ask Lee to call all our guests with reservations. We won't be able to serve dinner tonight. And please tell Loreen to send everyone home."

Shawn stayed in the kitchen with the firefighters while, outside in the dining room, Nancy found Bess talking to Elliot.

"Where is everybody?" Nancy asked.

"Loreen has them doing inventory downstairs," Bess said. "The sight of her staff standing around doing nothing drives her nuts."

"Loreen is actually quite nice," Elliot disagreed. "It's only lately that she's been, well, irritable."

"Do you know why?" Nancy asked him.

Elliot shook his head. "No, not really."

Remembering that she wanted to keep her identity as a detective secret, Nancy quickly controlled her impulse to barrage Elliot with questions.

Suddenly Elliot's face lit up. "I know where I've seen you before. I've been trying to figure it out all day. I saw your picture in the paper. You're Nancy Drew, the detective." He hunched his shoulders and leaned forward conspiratorially. "Are you investigating all the weird stuff that's been happening here?"

29

Nancy shook her head. "Just trying to earn some extra money, that's all."

"Really?" Elliot asked doubtfully.

"Sure," Nancy said lightly. "Please don't tell anyone about me, okay? I want to fit in here, and I'm willing to work hard and do my share."

"Your secret is safe with me," Elliot assured her.

Nancy gave Bess the message from Shawn about calling the reservations, and Bess went off to find the maître d'. "Now I have to tell Loreen to send everyone home," Nancy added with a sigh.

"I'll tell her," Elliot offered, getting up. "I have to talk to her about something else, anyway. I'll see you later."

As soon as he had gone, Bess reappeared. "I think you should drop this case, and I'm ready to quit the coatroom," she said to Nancy. "Whoever is doing all this stuff means business. We could have been killed in there."

Nancy nodded gravely. "I know. At first I thought it was a disgruntled employee playing pranks. But it's become a lot more serious than that."

"Then you'll give up the case?" Bess asked.

Nancy shook her head. "You know me. I can't give up just when things are beginning to heat up. I'd lie awake nights thinking about it, wondering who was responsible. Besides, I'd like to help Shawn, if I can."

"Which means I can't quit, either," Bess said with a sigh.

"It's okay with me if you want to," Nancy told her.

"Forget it," Bess scoffed. "I got you into this. I'm not leaving you all alone. Let me go help Lee cancel those reservations, and then we'll get out of here. I just want to go home and soak all of this soot out of my pores."

Nancy was about to follow Bess when she saw Shawn coming out of the kitchen. "I'll catch up with you in a minute," she told Bess.

"That was just what I needed," Shawn said, rubbing his eyes wearily. "Over a thousand dollars in fines."

"Ouch," Nancy sympathized. "Didn't you tell them you suspect arson?"

Shawn shook his head. "I decided not to. I don't need that kind of story getting around. If customers hear there's an arsonist with a gripe against this place, they'll never come here."

"I see your point," Nancy said. "Do the fire-fighters know how the fire started?"

"No, but they think it started with the linens in the cabinet," Shawn replied.

"Those linens burst into flame awfully fast," Nancy said, remembering that she and Bess had only stepped away for a minute or two when the fire started. "I'll bet they were soaked with something. I didn't smell gasoline, lighter fluid, or kerosene, though."

Shawn pushed one hand through his sandy hair

31

and sighed. "It's pretty mysterious, all right. Another attack from the phantom restaurant wrecker."

"It sure sounds that way," Nancy agreed.

Shawn ran his finger along a countertop. It came up black with soot. "What a day this has been," he said despondently, wiping his hand on a napkin. "I was counting on two things to make this place a success. One of them was good reviews. Then the biggest reviewer around, Harold Brackett, gets a mouthful of hot *wasabi* for lunch."

"He said he'd be back," Nancy reminded Shawn. "What else were you counting on?"

Shawn sighed. "The Dragon's Eye Ruby."

"The *what?*" Nancy asked.

Shawn pulled out a chair and sat down. "Don't you remember that monster ruby Gary Powell gave Stella Davis the third time they remarried?"

"I don't usually follow all that celebrity stuff," Nancy said, shaking her head.

"Well, this ruby is the granddaddy of all rubies," Shawn told her. "It's worth a fortune. When the couple divorced again, they sold the ruby. It was bought by Felice Wainwright."

"Really?" Nancy said, impressed. She'd never met Felice Wainwright, but she knew of her. Her aristocratic face and sleek blond hair frequently appeared in the society pages of the River Heights papers. She was one of the area's wealthiest women and lived in a Victorian mansion not far from the Arizona House.

"So how does the ruby fit into your plans?" Nancy asked.

"Well," Shawn replied, "it seems that Mrs. Wainwright has decided to auction off the ruby in order to fund some of her pet charities. Jewelers and anyone else interested in purchasing the ruby will be flying in from all over the country to attend the auction—along with the big preauction dinner Mrs. Wainwright is throwing this Saturday."

"And the dinner is being held here," Nancy supplied excitedly. "How wonderful for you."

Shawn sighed. "Yes, it could put the Arizona House on the map. But I'll be ruined if it's a disaster. And if things keep going the way they have, it *will* be a disaster. If Mrs. Wainwright gets wind of things, she might cancel the dinner, and that alone could drive me out of business. I've already ordered pounds of lobsters and cases of the finest champagne on credit, counting on the money from this dinner to pay the bill."

"I just read something about Felice Wainwright," Nancy said slowly, trying to remember what it was. "Didn't someone trip her alarm the other night?"

"I read that, too," Shawn said, nodding. "The intruder didn't get anything, and no one was caught. Maybe it was just a malfunction in the alarm. Rumor has it that Mrs. Wainwright had a super high-tech security system installed at her home just to protect the ruby."

Bess suddenly reappeared and joined Shawn and

Nancy. "Everybody's been called," she told Shawn. "Is it okay if Nancy and I leave?"

"Sure," he said. "See you ladies tomorrow. I have to go upstairs and make a few phone calls. I need to contact a professional clean-up crew right away. It'll be nearly impossible to get the smoke smell out of the restaurant." Shawn headed to the front hallway, where a stairway led to his office upstairs.

Bess turned to Nancy. "Can I get a lift from you?" she asked. "That way I won't have to bug Mom to come pick me up."

"Sure," Nancy said, wincing suddenly as she swallowed. "Did that smoke make your throat sore? Mine is killing me."

"Mine, too," Bess agreed as they walked toward the front door.

The girls were just about to leave when Bess stopped short. "Oh, I almost forgot the best part of this job! Today's payday. Shawn keeps our paychecks in his office. I'll be right back."

"I'll go with you," Nancy said. "It will give me a chance to see the upstairs."

Halfway up the narrow stairs, Nancy grabbed Bess by the arm. "Listen," she said. Raised voices were coming from the closed office door at the top of the stairs. "That sounds like Loreen."

Passing Bess, Nancy hurried toward the door and cocked her ear to listen. "Would you please calm down?" she heard Shawn say.

34

Loreen clearly had no intention of calming down. Her voice grew louder and more shrill with every word she spoke. "You've ruined my life with your lies," Loreen shouted angrily. "You'll be sorry you did all of this to me. I'll make you pay, Shawn Morgan, no matter what!"

4

Stakeout

Nancy stepped aside as the door suddenly swung open and Loreen stormed out. Barely noticing her or Bess, Loreen ran down the stairs.

"Loreen!" Shawn called from the doorway. Then, with a start, he realized Bess and Nancy were standing outside his office.

"Uh, I came for my pay," Bess said, smiling feebly.

"Sure, of course. Come on in," Shawn said, looking shaken.

"We couldn't help overhearing," Nancy said as she followed Bess into Shawn's small, plain office. "I thought you said Loreen had no reason to be angry at you?"

"She doesn't," Shawn insisted, sighing deeply. "Though I suppose she might think she does."

"What happened?" Nancy prodded.

Shawn shrugged. "She's still mad that I hired you."

Bess blinked. "All those fireworks over a new waitress?"

"There's a little more to it," Shawn admitted. "Loreen and I met when I was in culinary school out in Arizona. We fell in love and got engaged. She came to River Heights with me three months ago when I bought the restaurant. Loreen was a big help, and things were great for a while. Then I saw a side of Loreen I couldn't deal with."

"What side was that?" Nancy asked.

"Her insecure, jealous side," Shawn replied darkly. "Every time I hired a waitress, Loreen was sure I wanted to go out with her. Nothing I said could convince her it was strictly business."

"*Was* it always business?" Nancy asked. She smiled apologetically at Shawn's shocked expression. "Sorry, but I think I should know for the sake of the case."

"Always," Shawn said firmly. "Loreen had no reason for suspicion, but she drove me so crazy with her constant jealousy that I broke off the engagement."

"So that's why she's so angry," Bess filled in.

"I'm afraid so," Shawn said. "I've tried to make her see that it's best for both of us. We'll never be happy together if she doesn't trust me."

"Why does she stay on?" Nancy asked. "It must be uncomfortable for you both."

"She wants to go back to Arizona, but no one seems to be hiring out there right now. And Loreen doesn't know anyone in River Heights besides me. All her family and friends are in Arizona. I think she's saving up to go back. That's one of the reasons I don't have the heart to fire her. Besides, Loreen's a great head waitress. For three months, she's put all her energy into helping me get set up." Shawn sighed. "I know she still thinks of this restaurant as part hers. It would have been if we married."

"Is Loreen angry enough to destroy your business?" Nancy asked pointedly.

"I really don't think so," Shawn replied. "Loreen isn't the vengeful type, despite what you may have just heard."

"On the other hand," Bess pointed out, "she has the chance to destroy the place from inside."

Nancy nodded. "Where was Loreen before and during the fire?" she asked Shawn.

"She was in my office from the time you spoke to her until just before the fire," Shawn answered.

Bess looked at Nancy. "That *would* make it hard for her to set a fire."

"True," Nancy had to admit. "I'll just have to keep my eyes open and see what turns up. Is there anyone else who might have a grudge against you? What about Jack or Elliot?"

"Why are you asking about them?" Shawn questioned.

"They were the last ones in the kitchen before the fire," Nancy reminded him.

Shawn's eyes wandered to the ceiling as he thought. "Elliot . . . no. I can't think of any reason. And I did Jack a favor when I gave him the job. He needed work. So I don't think he would be angry with me. Just the opposite, really."

"I guess I'll have to keep my eyes open, then," Nancy concluded.

"I appreciate all of this," Shawn said, handing Bess her pay envelope.

At that moment, Roy came to the door. "Shawn, I wanted you to know something," the bartender said. "When Loreen had us doing inventory, I discovered that I'm short two bottles of vodka. Somebody's pilfering your liquor."

"What next?" Shawn groaned, shaking his head.

Nancy suddenly felt weary. The smoke she'd inhaled had given her a headache, and the soreness in her throat was growing worse. After Roy left, she said, "I'll get to the bottom of this tomorrow. Right now, I think I need to rest."

"Good idea," Shawn agreed. "See you then."

Bess and Nancy went down the stairs and headed out to the parking lot. As Nancy slipped behind the steering wheel, she couldn't believe how much had happened in so little time. It was only a quarter to seven and still light outside.

"So what do you make of all this?" Bess asked, strapping herself into the passenger seat.

"Right now, it could be anybody," Nancy said as she started the car. "Maybe Shawn himself has been doing these things."

"No way!" Bess cried.

"If he's in financial trouble, he might set fire to his own place to collect the insurance money," Nancy said with a shrug. "Or maybe he's setting this whole thing up so that if he *does* torch the restaurant, it will look like this mystery culprit is responsible."

"Shawn is the sweetest guy, Nancy. How can you suspect him?" Bess said, frowning.

Nancy pulled the car out of the lot. "Bess, I'm sorry, but everyone is a suspect until the case is solved. You know that."

As Nancy headed toward Bess's house, neither she nor Bess spoke. Both girls were lost in their private thoughts.

Then Bess began to talk about George Fayne, her cousin and Nancy's good friend. "It's too bad George isn't here," Bess said. "She usually has some good ideas. I hope she's having fun on that camping trip." She shuddered. "Hiking through the wilderness sounds like torture to me, but George was actually excited about it, can you believe it. . . ."

As Bess went on, Nancy was only half listening. Something was bothering her, like a gentle tapping on her brain. "The vodka!" she suddenly exclaimed.

"What?" Bess asked, her brows furrowed.

"If someone threw vodka on those linens and then lit them, they'd go right up in flames. And vodka has a mild smell. It would be hard to detect."

"Oh, you mean the missing vodka," Bess said, catching on.

"The linens would have had to be soaked right before the fire. Then the culprit would simply have to walk by and toss in a match," Nancy went on.

"Sounds like a good theory to me," Bess agreed. "Wouldn't a person dumping vodka on linens be pretty obvious, though?"

"Not if they did it right after Jack and Elliot left. We were busy in the back, and there was no one else in the kitchen," Nancy pointed out. "Or Jack could have done it after Elliot left."

"Jack and Elliot could be working together," Bess suggested. "But Elliot doesn't seem the type. Jack does, though. What a grouch!"

As she continued to drive, Nancy noticed the Wainwright mansion sitting high atop a hill. She recognized it from a picture she'd seen in the River Heights newspaper. Gabled roofs and two rounded towers topped the third floor. On the bottom floor was a wraparound porch. Small balconies adorned the second floor windows. Although the house was over one hundred years old, it was well kept, with a fresh coat of white paint and manicured landscaping.

"Wouldn't you just love to be super rich?" Bess asked with a sigh as they drove past.

"I guess," Nancy said, never having given the idea much thought. Then she filled Bess in on what Shawn had told her about the Dragon's Eye Ruby.

"You'd better get to the bottom of this mystery

41

fast," Bess said as Nancy pulled up in front of the Marvins' house. "Shawn will be ruined for sure if Saturday night's dinner is a flop."

"I know," Nancy agreed. "It sounds as if he's in over his head. The only way to bail him out is by solving this case before Saturday. And it's already Tuesday night."

After Nancy had dropped off Bess, she continued home. The house was empty, cool, and quiet. Hannah Gruen, the housekeeper who had lived with the Drews since Nancy's mother had died when she was a child, had taken the week off to visit a friend in Chicago. As usual, Carson Drew was working late at the office.

Nancy showered, then crawled into bed and fell asleep. When she awoke a few hours later, the red digital numbers on her clock said ten-fifteen. Pulling on her robe, Nancy went downstairs, where she found her father reading on the couch in the living room.

"Are you okay?" he asked when he saw Nancy. "It's not like you to take a nap."

Nancy sat down and told him all that had gone on earlier that evening in the restaurant. "The smoke made me a little sick, but I feel fine now."

"Be careful, Nancy," her father said, frowning. "This person isn't fooling around."

"I'll use extra caution," she assured him.

Carson put down his paper and reached over to the table beside the couch. "This evening, when I got home, I dug this out to show you." He handed Nancy a faded yellow menu.

Nancy studied the front cover. On it was a sketch of a brick building. Striped canopies adorned the windows, and an ornate wooden door graced the main entrance. Written across the top of the menu were the words Chez Jacques. "This is a picture of the Arizona House, right?" Nancy asked in surprise.

"Back when it was Chez Jacques," Carson said. "It looks pretty different, I guess."

"I can see that Shawn's made a lot of changes," Nancy agreed. "Why do you have this?"

Carson shrugged. "Oh, it was some fancy law association dinner. Your mother had it tucked away in a scrapbook."

Nancy opened the menu and looked at the prices. "This must have been the cheapest place in town."

Her father laughed. "It was the fanciest, most expensive place in town. Those were high prices in those days."

Turning the menu over, Nancy saw a black and white photo of a man on the back cover. He was short but handsome, with a full head of dark hair. Above his picture it said "Jacques Henri wishes his customers *bon appetit!*"

Nancy studied the photo. Something about the man's face had caught her attention. His dark, intense eyes seemed to bore right into her.

"It's Jack," she said finally, looking up at her

43

father. "I met him today. He's the dessert chef. He's much older now, but I'm sure this is him."

Carson Drew took the menu from Nancy. "Now that you mention it, I believe Chez Jacques was famous for its great desserts."

"Hmmm," Nancy mused, sitting down on the couch. "And now the tables have turned, and Jack is working for someone else. I wonder why he no longer owns the restaurant?"

"I'm sure you'll find out tomorrow," said her father, kissing her lightly on the forehead. "Now I'm going to bed. You're sure you feel all right?"

"Fine," she answered. "Good night, Dad."

Nancy sat up on the couch and continued to gaze at the menu. Her short nap had restored her energy. Now she was restless and eager to solve this case. "I won't be able to sleep, anyway," she told herself as she got off the couch and hurried up to her room.

In minutes, she had pulled on a pair of black leggings, a long-sleeved black top, and a pair of black high-top sneakers. Tying her hair back with a wide black band, she checked her image in the mirror. "Dressed for a stakeout," she said with a grin. Nancy buckled a small black leather pouch around her waist and put in her wallet, car keys, a lock-picking kit, and a pocket flashlight.

Downstairs, Nancy left her father a note, then headed out the door to her car.

Nancy drove as quickly as the speed limit allowed. Within ten minutes, she pulled into the parking lot of the Arizona House, just as Shawn was driving out from the back lot in his white compact station wagon. "What are you doing here?" he asked, pulling up alongside her.

Nancy realized she'd miscalculated. She had expected the restaurant to be empty by eleven, especially since there'd been no dinner seating. "I thought I'd come by and just watch the place for a while," she said. "I wanted to see if anyone showed up. Aren't you here sort of late?"

"I was working with the cleanup crew," Shawn replied. "They all left about ten minutes ago. What a job! But we'll be able to open for lunch tomorrow."

Nancy shut off the ignition and climbed out of her car. "Shawn, what can you tell me about Jack?"

"Jack?" Shawn echoed. "Well, as you may have already discovered, Jack used to own this place. He and my father were partners, actually. When Dad died, Jack couldn't manage alone. He's not really a businessman. The place went into a slide. I inherited Dad's half of the restaurant, but I was too young to help out then. Three months ago, when I got out of culinary school, I made Jack an offer to buy out his half of the business. The restaurant had closed and had been up for sale for three years. By the time I came along, Jack was out of money. I couldn't pay top dollar, but in the long run Jack accepted my offer and sold me his half."

"Why is he working for you?" Nancy asked.

"He's the greatest pastry and dessert chef

45

around," Shawn explained. "He needed a job, and I was glad to have him. Why? Do you suspect him?"

"Everybody's a suspect to me," Nancy said with a smile. "Why didn't you tell me all this before?"

"You asked if anyone had a grudge against me," Shawn reminded her, "and Jack doesn't. I think he was relieved to get the old restaurant off his hands." Shawn folded his arms and looked at Nancy sharply. "What exactly were you hoping to accomplish tonight?"

"Whoever is harassing you could be getting in at night," she replied. "So I thought I'd hide my car in the back, behind the dumpster, then wait to see if anyone shows up. But since you're still here, you can let me inside. That's even better."

"No way," Shawn said firmly. "It's too dangerous."

"I'll hide," Nancy said with a shrug. "The person won't even see me. That's why I'm dressed in black," she added.

"I thought you were just being chic," Shawn teased.

"Very funny," Nancy said with a wry smile. "So, you'll let me in?"

"No. In fact, I insist you go home. I don't want you hanging out in the parking lot, either. Catch this person in the daylight with lots of people around. Not alone in the dark."

Nancy could see Shawn wasn't budging from his position. Still, she was determined to get into that restaurant. "All right," she said, pretending to give in. "But as long as I'm here, I left my sweater inside, in the coatroom—mind if I get it?"

"Of course not," Shawn said, getting out of his car and walking with her to the door. Taking a set of keys from his jacket pocket, he unlocked it. "Want me to turn on some lights?" he offered.

"No, I'm okay," Nancy said, stepping into the dark restaurant. "It's just in the coatroom."

"I'll wait for you by my car," Shawn called as he headed toward the parking lot.

"Okay," Nancy said, shutting the door. Earlier that evening, with the trained instincts of an experienced detective, she had noted that the front door could be set to lock automatically when the door was pulled shut. Just as she'd suspected, the lock was set to close by itself. With a click, she turned the rectangular metal piece on the lock so that the door would stay unlocked when she closed it behind her.

A few moments later, Nancy came out of the restaurant. "It's not there," she told Shawn, who was leaning on the hood of his car. "I was wrong."

"Just shut the door," Shawn said. "It will lock behind you."

Nancy shut the door, then headed to her Mustang. "See you tomorrow," she said.

"Good night," Shawn replied, getting into his car.

Nancy pulled away first. When she was about a half mile from the restaurant, she shut off her lights and pulled into a dark drive that led to an abandoned barn. Crouched low in her seat, Nancy waited. In a few moments, Shawn drove past.

When he was safely down the road, Nancy flicked her headlights back on and headed toward the restaurant once again.

Pulling into the lot behind the Arizona House, Nancy hid her car in back of a large garbage dumpster. It was a dark night. Nancy looked up at the sky and saw that clouds covered the moon and stars. Thinking it was safe to cut across the parking lot, Nancy ran toward the restaurant.

She was halfway across the lot, and there wasn't another person in sight. The only sound was the leaves rustling in the breeze.

Suddenly, a brilliant light flashed in her eyes.

Nancy gasped and stood still, blinded by the light.

5

Night Visitors

Nancy shielded her eyes with her hand, then looked around sharply, braced for anything. Her heart was pounding as she searched the parking lot. Ahead of her, she found the source of the blinding light. A large floodlight was mounted at the corner of the restaurant.

"A motion-detector light," Nancy told herself, letting her breath out in a whoosh of relief. The light had a sensor that detected any movement. It went on automatically when anyone approached.

Nancy backed out of the light's field and was again enveloped in darkness as the bulb snapped off. Quickly, she ran to the front of the building and slipped in through the open door. She listened a minute and heard nothing but the low hum of an ice-making machine in the lounge. The restaurant was quiet and apparently empty.

Nancy knew she should find a place to hide, in

case someone did show up. The dining room would be a central location. Her eyes soon adjusted to the darkness, and she found her way into the dining room without using her flashlight.

Suddenly there was a huge crash!

Nancy's heart leaped into her throat. She stood, frozen. The sound had come from the kitchen.

Regaining her composure, Nancy quietly made her way to the kitchen door and cautiously pushed it open. Peering in, she saw only a silent kitchen gently illuminated by the red glow of the exit sign above the back door.

Just then, Nancy gasped and jumped back. A small dark shadow had scurried right past her feet. A mouse, she realized. She knew that a mouse, drawn by the smell of food, could make its way into the cleanest of kitchens. Still, Nancy was surprised. Shawn's kitchen was so spotless, and all of the food was stored away efficiently.

Peering into the darkness, she saw something lying on the floor near one of the counters. It looked like a box of some kind.

Nancy cocked her head and listened hard. There was no sign of life in the kitchen. If someone had been there, he or she could have run out the back door. Nancy took her penlight from her leather pouch and aimed it on the box. It was actually a crudely made mesh cage about the size of a small microwave oven. The crash she'd heard must have been the cage falling from the counter. Had it been set too precariously at the edge? Or had someone jostled it?

Summoning her nerve, Nancy stepped into the dark kitchen and flashed her light around the room. It seemed empty. A chill suddenly ran up Nancy's arm. Looking to her right, she saw that the door to the large steel walk-in refrigerator was open.

Instantly, Nancy snapped off her penlight. Perhaps the culprit was busy inside and hadn't even noticed her light. Quietly, she crept toward the open door, then stood behind it and listened.

Scritch-scritch-scratch.

A strange scuffling, scratching sound was all Nancy heard. Carefully, she peeked around the corner. The refrigerator was loaded with crates of fruits, vegetables, dairy products, and other supplies. No one appeared to be inside. Yet the scuffling sound continued.

Once again snapping on her penlight, Nancy saw three mice gnawing at a large net bag of apples. The minute her light shone on them, they scurried away, disappearing behind the crates, boxes, and bags that lined the walls.

Nancy stepped into the doorway. The walk-in fridge was the size of a small room, but it was crammed with supplies, leaving very little room for a person to move around inside.

"Of course," Nancy said out loud as she continued to sweep her light around the refrigerator. It made sense, all right. This was the latest sabotage.

Someone had released mice in the kitchen and left this door open.

It was perfect. Not only would the mice destroy the restaurant's food supplies, but Shawn would have to close down while an exterminator rid his place of the rodents.

Suddenly a warning chill shot up Nancy's spine. She could feel that someone was close by. But before Nancy could even turn, two strong hands closed over her shoulders and shoved her into the refrigerator. The force of the action sent her crashing to her knees.

Slam! The refrigerator door swung shut.

Nancy scrambled to her feet and threw her weight against the inside handle. The door wouldn't budge. "Hey!" she called to her attacker. "Let me out of here!"

Her cries were met with deadly silence.

Panic gripped Nancy for a moment, but she quickly pushed it away. There's got to be a way *out* of here, Nancy thought as she scanned the walls and ceiling with her flashlight. Her beam shone on a small red button with the word "alarm" written on it.

Climbing onto a crate of tomatoes, Nancy reached up and pressed the button. A clattering ring sounded outside the refrigerator. She pressed her thumb into the button and held it there. The ring persisted, but no one came.

This is dumb, Nancy decided, lowering herself

off the crate. The only one who can hear this alarm is the person who pushed me in here.

Nancy blew on her hands for warmth. A smoky cloud of breath formed in the air. Her cotton shirt and leggings were no protection against this kind of extreme cold. Her teeth were already chattering.

And then there was the question of air. Nancy wasn't sure how much she had left in the small space. She was sure of one thing, though. By the time someone found her the next morning, she would be in pretty bad shape. That was, if there was enough air to get her through the night.

A sound in the corner made Nancy jump. The mice, she remembered. Normally, she wasn't squeamish about the furry little creatures. But being locked in such small quarters with them was a different story. She'd have to try not to think about it.

A mouse ran quickly across the floor and darted behind a crate. She'd have to try very hard.

Settling uncomfortably on the edge of another crate, Nancy tried to formulate a plan. She'd been in tough spots before. And if she'd learned anything, it was to stay calm and think clearly. If she let panic get the better of her, it would be all over.

Just then the door handle clicked. Nancy's nerves tingled as she stepped back, preparing to confront whoever stepped through the door.

With a creak, the heavy door fell open a crack, but no one appeared. Nancy realized someone was letting her out but was not going to show him or herself. He or she might be sneaking out of the kitchen right now.

"Stop!" Nancy cried, bounding out of the refrigerator.

A shadowy figure was already near the back of the kitchen. A moment later, Nancy heard the door slam as the culprit dashed outside.

Racing across the kitchen, Nancy pulled the door open in time to see a man caught in the beam of the motion detector light. For a second she saw him— short and broad-shouldered with a dark knit hat covering his hair. In the next moment, he ran out of the light's field. The light snapped off, and he was engulfed in darkness.

Nancy chased him out into the lot. The light snapped on as she stood beneath it, and she could see that the lot was empty. No car engine sounded. The man seemed to have disappeared into the night air.

A fat raindrop hit Nancy's brow, and a sprinkling of drops began to fall around her. She turned and went back into the restaurant. She had to call Shawn and tell him what she'd discovered. Someone had to catch those mice!

Deciding to use the phone in Shawn's office, Nancy headed across the dining room and up the stairs.

Inside the office, she clicked on the overhead light, then made her way to the phone. Fortunately, Shawn's number was one of five numbers listed on his instant-dial machine. Three other numbers belonged to food, linen, and beverage suppliers. The fourth was marked Loreen.

Nancy hit the button marked Home, and the phone automatically dialed Shawn. "Hello, this is Shawn. I can't come to the phone right now . . ." his answering machine responded.

Nancy spoke when the machine's tone sounded. "Shawn, this is Nancy. There's trouble at the restaurant. I'll wait for you here another half hour. After that, call me at home."

She left her number, hung up the phone, and settled into Shawn's swiveling leather office chair. I've seen that man who ran from the kitchen before, she mused. Yet she couldn't remember where.

Resting her head back on the chair, Nancy closed her eyes. She let the image of the man running through the parking lot play through her head. She saw his shoulders, his black shirt, his knit hat.

This mental instant replay revealed something to her that she'd missed. She had seen the man's sideburns and the back of his hair. His hair was silvery gray.

Nancy's eyes flew open. "Jack!" It wasn't just the hair. It was his build, his way of moving, everything. She was sure it was him.

"Case closed," she said, getting out of the chair. "Almost." She still needed a motive. It probably had something to do with Shawn's deal with Jack. Maybe Jack thought Shawn had underpaid him and he was getting even. Perhaps there were bad feelings between Shawn and Jack, something Shawn was too embarrassed to reveal.

Nancy was no longer content to sit and wait for Shawn. Why wasn't he home? Maybe he was home but had gone to sleep. Nancy debated driving to his house and waking him up. Surely he'd want to know what she'd uncovered.

Turning off the light, Nancy headed back down the stairs. As she opened the front door, she saw that the rainstorm was in full fury, spattering the front lot with its driving torrents.

Nancy was about to dash to her car when she remembered the open refrigerator door. There was no sense letting all Shawn's food spoil.

Closing the front door gently, she turned back toward the kitchen. A clap of thunder exploded overhead, followed by the flash of jagged lightning in the windows.

In that split second of brightness, Nancy spotted another dark figure in the dining room!

Nancy flattened herself against the hallway wall. Her heart was hammering in her ears as she wondered if the intruder had heard her. She hoped that the thunder and rain had masked the sound of her footsteps.

Moving soundlessly, she made her way to the entrance of the dining room and crouched low, near the reservations stand.

The person inside the dark dining room was staring at one of the paintings on the wall. His eyes had obviously adjusted to the darkness, since he didn't use a light. From the man's height alone, Nancy could tell it was not Jack. This person was of medium build. Baggy clothing disguised the rest of the physical outline, though Nancy was fairly sure that it was a man.

What was going on? Why was the intruder standing there like that?

Then, with one startlingly swift gesture, the figure raised his arm. Nancy saw the glimmer of the knife in his hand as it swung over his head—then slashed through the painting's canvas!

Again and again the man pierced the painting with his knife. Then he began to slash the painting beside it.

Alone in the dark, Nancy knew it would be foolish to confront an intruder with a knife. Instead, she would have to follow him—preferably from the safety of her car.

Then a horrible thought hit her. What if Shawn showed up? He might run into the knife-wielding intruder. Nancy shuddered. She had no choice but to wait outside. That way she could intercept Shawn, or be ready to tail the intruder as soon as he got into his car.

Stealthily, Nancy made her way back to the front door. She slipped through and ran out into the pouring rain. Splattering through puddles, she raced around to the windowless side of the building.

There, parked by the building, was a compact black sedan. Obviously the intruder had expected to be alone at this hour. She noted the license plate: RV5-289. There was no time to investigate any further. She ran to the dumpster, glad she'd thought to hide her car away behind it.

Thunder clapped overhead as Nancy stood behind the dumpster and peered around it. What a night! she thought, shaking her head wearily as the rain soaked her clothing. A few minutes later, the man emerged from the front of the building and got into his car. Nancy hoped a flash of lightning would shed some light on him, but it didn't come quickly enough. The storm was beginning to move away.

As soon as the man turned on his ignition, Nancy got into her Mustang. She pulled out from behind the dumpster in time to see him heading up the dirt road away from the Arizona House. She decided to risk leaving her headlights off as they traveled along the road. Accelerating slightly, she followed the red points of his taillights through the rain.

After half a mile, the car turned into a more residential section. Nancy slowed and fell back. She'd have to turn on her lights now or risk being stopped by the police. It was late, and there were hardly any other cars on the road. Nancy knew she would need to stay well behind to avoid being spotted.

The car's driver didn't seem to be in any hurry. That was a good sign. He didn't realize she was following him. Nancy tailed him past the expensive homes in the area and was surprised when the car slowed down and stopped in front of the Wainwright estate.

What was he looking for? What connection did the Wainwright estate have with this man? But just as the thoughts flashed through Nancy's mind, she realized she had a more pressing problem. How was she going to avoid being noticed now?

She had no other choice. She continued driving past the car and made a right into the first available cross street, several yards ahead. Nancy pulled to the curb and cut her lights. She would have to wait for the car to pass before she could tail it again.

Nancy had to wait five minutes before the sedan passed. This time, its tires squealed as it raced down the street. Startled, Nancy could barely start her car fast enough. Though she was still within the speed limit, Nancy didn't like to drive so fast in a storm. Her wipers slapped furiously, sending rivers of water streaming off the sides of her car. Her hands gripped the wheel as she concentrated on keeping control of the car.

Was the intruder now trying to shake her tail? It seemed so. Nancy let up on the gas. If she fell back a little, maybe he would think she was gone. She'd risk losing him, but it was a risk worth taking.

The sedan turned onto the highway that ran along the outskirts of River Heights. Nancy followed it. On the open road, the sedan sped even faster, but the conditions made it easier for Nancy to keep track of the car, even at a distance. She saw it turn off at the exit leading into the seediest section of River Heights.

A traffic light at the end of the exit had slowed the sedan's progress, and Nancy was in time to see it turn right at the light. She caught the green light and regained sight of the car, which was about a block ahead of her.

The storm was slowing to a drizzle now. Nancy followed the sedan for two more dark, shabby blocks. Without warning, the sedan turned sharply into a brightly lit twenty-four-hour drive-through car wash.

A car wash? Nancy thought, puzzled.

Forgetting caution, Nancy pulled into the lot just as the sedan disappeared behind the cloth flaps that dangled over the car wash entrance. She had him now. When the car emerged under the bright spotlight, Nancy would be waiting, ready to get a clear view of the driver. She might even confront him. It would be safer out in the open.

Without hesitating, Nancy drove past the confused attendant. She parked her car around front, blocking the exit of the car wash. She waited. Slowly, the front end of the black sedan emerged, riding on the washer conveyor belt.

Newly washed and waxed, the hood gleamed. Finally, the windshield emerged. Nancy stared into the car through the glistening glass.

The car was empty.

6

Missing Pieces

Nancy waited. She was sure the driver was merely crouched in his seat. He wouldn't stay there forever.

Three minutes passed, and Nancy couldn't stand to wait any longer. Keeping low, she left her car and crept alongside the sedan to a rear window. She carefully peeked into the car. The keys were still in the ignition, but the car was completely empty!

Nancy moved to the trunk. It was locked. Just to be sure, she grabbed the keys from the ignition and opened the trunk. Empty.

He's still in the car wash, Nancy decided, sprinting to the entrance.

"Hey, lady!" cried the attendant as Nancy brushed aside the heavy cloth flaps covering the opening. "You can't go in there."

Ignoring the attendant, Nancy ran into the center of the dark, dripping car wash.

"Lady, are you nuts?" asked the short, thin attendant as he came into the car wash behind her.

"The man who drove that car, where is he?" Nancy asked urgently.

The attendant shrugged. "Isn't he in his car?"

"No," Nancy replied. "Is there a light in here?"

The attendant stepped to the side and flipped a switch. The garagelike room, filled with hoses, sprayers, and brushes, was suddenly bright. Nancy and the attendant were clearly the only ones inside.

"You must have seen the man when he paid you," Nancy said. "What did he look like?"

The attendant's eyes narrowed suspiciously. "You mean, you don't even know this guy?"

"I'm a detective. I was trailing him," Nancy explained. "What does he look like?"

The attendant folded his arms. "Hard to say. He had on dark glasses, which was weird, since it's nighttime. But we get all kinds of crazies in this neighborhood."

"What color hair?" Nancy urged.

"I don't know. He had on a tweed cap, I think."

"Any scars, a mustache, *anything?*" Nancy asked.

"Hey, I'm no FBI agent," the attendant replied irritably. "I don't inspect the customers. I just take their money and pass them through. He was a guy wearing sunglasses and a cap. That's all I know."

"He must have slipped out the back," Nancy told herself, walking to the rear entrance. Behind the car wash was a low fence, which surrounded a row of tall warehouse buildings with unlit alleys. Nancy guessed that the driver had hopped the fence and disappeared down one of the alleys.

It was now obvious to Nancy that he'd realized she was following him. Her ploy of hanging back hadn't worked.

"What am I supposed to do with his car?" asked the attendant, coming up behind Nancy.

She threw him the keys. "Pull it to the side. I'm going to contact the police. They'll come pick it up. If the driver returns, please call me right away. My name is Nancy Drew, and I'm listed in the phone book. And try to get a good look at him if he comes back, okay?"

"Will do," the attendant said with a shrug.

"Thanks," Nancy said as she headed back to her car.

"Hey, wait!" the attendant called. "I just remembered something. The guy had strange hands. They looked kind of like plastic."

"Thanks," Nancy called back again as she climbed into her Mustang. Surgical gloves, she thought. They could be bought at any surgical supply store. That meant there wouldn't be a single fingerprint anywhere.

As Nancy drove back onto the highway, she looked at her watch. It was one in the morning. It was a good thing she had taken a nap. Besides, she was now super-charged from the excitement.

Dark glasses and a tweed cap, she thought, mulling over the attendant's description. She was fairly sure he hadn't worn those at the restaurant.

He must have had them in the car and put them on to avoid being recognized in any way by the attendant. It seemed she was dealing with a quick-thinking adversary.

Nancy pulled into a highway gas station and used the pay phone to call Shawn. Once again, his machine answered, but this time he'd recorded a message for her: "Nancy. I got your message. I'm at the restaurant. Please come down or call me as soon as you hear this."

In about ten minutes Nancy was back at the Arizona House. The restaurant was completely lit up. This time she pulled into the front lot right next to Shawn's car and a River Heights police car.

As soon as she walked through the front door Shawn hurried to meet her. He was dressed in jeans and a sport shirt, and his hair was mussed, as if he'd run out the minute he got her message.

"What happened here?" he asked.

"I'm not a hundred percent sure," Nancy admitted, moving into the dining room. All of the restaurant's paintings had been slashed and thrown to the floor. One wall had been badly vandalized with swirling black lines of spray paint. Two uniformed officers were busy making note of the damage.

"Here's what I do know," Nancy said, turning to Shawn. She recounted all the night's events, from the mice in the kitchen to the empty black sedan at the car wash.

"How did you get into the restaurant?" Shawn asked.

Nancy admitted her ruse.

"You could have suffocated in that walk-in refrigerator, you know," Shawn scolded. "Not to mention that you were in here with some knife-wielding lunatic. I told you to go home, remember?"

"I'm all right. I was only trying to solve this case," Nancy defended herself. "At least now we have a few clues."

Shawn smiled wanly. "Okay. You win. I'm glad you're all right. Now, what clues do we have?"

"Well, I'm almost positive that the guy who let the mice loose is Jack," she told him.

Shawn raised his eyebrows. "I can't believe that."

"Sorry. But it sure looked like him," Nancy said gently. "Either you have two vandals working separately, or Jack is working with the other guy. But I don't think he is. Jack would have told the other guy I was here. Besides, the second guy would have heard the commotion in the kitchen if he'd been here with Jack. He didn't, though, which means he came in while I was upstairs in the office."

"But why would either one of them do this to me?" Shawn asked.

"Shawn," Nancy said, "were you honest with me when you said Jack had no reason to be angry?"

"Yes," Shawn insisted. "I made him an offer for the restaurant, and he accepted it. I even gave him a job. Why should he be angry?"

"I don't know," Nancy admitted. "Well, at least we have a good chance of finding the slasher. The police can run a registration check on the license plate number."

"Don't tell the police about Jack yet, all right?" Shawn urged her. "I don't want to say anything until we're sure. He goes back so far with my family."

Nancy hesitated, then said, "Okay."

Nancy told the police about the vandal and how she'd tailed him to the car wash. Immediately, one of the officers, a tall, young, blond man, went to the phone to call his precinct for a check on the car.

"This has been a long day," Shawn said, stifling a yawn. "Want some coffee?"

"Do you have hot chocolate?" Nancy asked.

"Of course. This is a restaurant, remember?" Shawn said with a smile. "I'll be right back."

While he was gone, Nancy studied the paintings that the police had laid out on the tables. Five of them had been slashed on a crisp diagonal. But the sixth one—a large oil landscape of a lake surrounded by woods—had been attacked with particular vengeance. Entire pieces of the painting had been gouged out.

Curious, Nancy knelt down on the floor next to the wall that had held the paintings. One at a time, she retrieved the small pieces of canvas that had fluttered to the floor. She continued to collect them until she had a small handful of pieces.

Slowly and precisely, Nancy fit the pieces into the tattered framework of the painting as though they were bits of a jigsaw puzzle.

"What are you doing?" Shawn asked, placing a steaming mug on the table beside her.

"This painting took a particular beating," Nancy answered without looking up from her work. "I wanted to see if I recognized the location." Finally, she looked up and took a sip of her hot chocolate. "Thanks," she said to Shawn. "Did you check your refrigerator? The door has been open for a while, I'm afraid. Sorry. I was about to close it when I spotted the second intruder."

"The food hasn't spoiled yet, but tomorrow I'm going to have to go through everything and see what the mice have gotten into," Shawn said grimly. "According to health department regulations, I have to toss anything they've touched. I'll have to get an exterminator in the morning." Shawn sighed. "Let's just say this is a complete disaster. If this keeps up, I don't know what's going to happen with the auction dinner. What a nightmare!"

"I'm really sorry all this is happening to you," Nancy said sympathetically.

"You're doing more than I could have expected," Shawn said. He looked down at the painting. "So? Do you recognize the place?"

Nancy shook her head. "I'm still missing a big triangular piece right here on the lower left." She went back to the area near the wall and searched some more. "It doesn't seem to be here at all," she noted.

"It has to be," Shawn said. He helped her look,

but after five minutes, they'd still turned up nothing. "That's strange," Shawn murmured.

Nancy returned to the assembled pieces and studied them. "You know what else is strange? Look how precisely this missing piece was cut. All these other pieces are torn and ragged, but not this section." She outlined the missing shape with her finger. "It looks as though it was cut out with a razor." She gazed up at Shawn. "Do you remember what was in this section?"

"Not exactly," Shawn said. "I think it was just more trees. Does this mean anything to you?"

Nancy drummed the table thoughtfully with her fingertips. "Something isn't adding up here. Why can't we find the piece of this painting?"

"You really think it's important?" Shawn asked skeptically.

"Maybe not," Nancy admitted. "Where did these paintings come from?"

"I bought them from Felice Wainwright," Shawn replied.

"Felice Wainwright!" Nancy exclaimed, remembering the way the sedan had slowed outside the heiress's estate. "Why did you say you bought them from a friend?"

Embarrassed, Shawn stared down at the floor. "I didn't want to admit I was playing up to Mrs. Wainwright. As you might know, Mrs. Wainwright is involved in all sorts of charity work," Shawn went on. "Her pet project is an art program for model prisoners, and she kind of pressured me into buying these for the restaurant."

"You didn't really want them?" Nancy asked.

Shawn shrugged. "They're okay, I guess, but they don't exactly go with the decor."

"Then why did you buy them?" Nancy asked.

"Well, we were discussing the booking for her preauction dinner. She was telling me how, if things went well, she'd recommend the Arizona House to all her friends. And then, in the same breath, she asked if I was interested in buying a bunch of paintings by this prisoner named Joseph Spaziente. He's in her art class, and I guess he's her big discovery. She thinks he's some kind of artistic genius. I couldn't say no—and she knew it, too."

Just then, one of the officers joined them. He was a short, husky man with dark hair. "Here's my report," he said, placing a clipboard on the table in front of Shawn. "Is there anything you'd like to add?"

Shawn glanced over the report. "I don't think so. The main damage is to the wall and the seven paintings."

"Seven?" Nancy asked. "I only see six."

Shawn looked at the paintings laid out on the table. "There's the seventh, over there," he said, pointing to a large, severely slashed oil landscape still leaning against the wall.

"It looks like it's the same scene as this one with the missing triangle," Nancy observed.

Shawn shrugged. "I think it is, but it shows a different season."

Before Nancy could examine the seventh painting, the tall, blond officer returned. "That sedan you followed was reported stolen this morning. It's registered to an elderly woman named Sarah Glass. She says that her car disappeared while she was eating at a coffee shop. Her keys were gone from her purse, too."

"The thief probably watched her park, then followed her inside to pickpocket her keys," Nancy said, frowning.

"Good thinking, little lady," said the policeman. "You should be a detective."

Nancy smiled politely.

"We can have the car dusted for prints," the other officer suggested.

"It won't help," Nancy told them. "He was wearing surgical gloves."

"So we're at a dead end," Shawn said.

"We'll be leaving now," said the blond officer. "Call us if anything new develops. We'll be looking for this guy, but we don't have much of a description to go on."

"Thanks for your time, officers," Shawn said, escorting the two men to the door.

Nancy stayed behind to examine the seventh painting. It, too, had taken a worse beating than the other five. It was a summer scene, showing swimmers wading in a lake. As Nancy had noted, it showed the same landscape as the other painting, rendered from exactly the same perspective, but in a different season. The first lake scene was set in spring, with blossoming trees.

Nancy knelt on the floor and replaced the scattered pieces, smoothing them with her hand. Then she studied her work and gasped.

A perfect triangle had also been cut from the summer scene—in exactly the same spot as in the spring painting. And that triangle, too, was gone!

7

A Startling Appearance

Throughout the night, Nancy wrestled with the question of the missing triangles. She tossed and turned in her bed, unable to fall asleep despite the late hour.

The triangles had to mean something. It was just too coincidental. Nancy's every instinct as a detective told her there was more to this case than there seemed. But what?

The slashed paintings had all been done by one artist, who was a prisoner. Why would someone want two triangles cut from those paintings? Nancy didn't like the prison connection. It spelled trouble to her.

By ten o'clock Wednesday morning, Nancy had showered, eaten breakfast, and dressed for work at the Arizona House. Part of her wanted to sleep in till the afternoon, but another part was eager to pursue the case.

The night before, Shawn had walked Nancy to her car. On the way out he'd told her he was determined to clean the place up in time for lunch, even if it meant staying up all night.

The Arizona House lunch staff wasn't expected at work until eleven, but Nancy arrived there by ten-thirty. She parked in the back lot, beside Shawn's white compact station wagon.

The back door was locked, so Nancy walked around to the front. The door stood ajar. Nancy entered and found Shawn in the lounge, counting money at the register behind the bar.

When he saw her, he smiled. "I just put two hundred dollars into the register so Roy will have money for change. As long as I have two hundred to put in each day, I'm not going out of business."

"Good attitude," Nancy said with a grin. She couldn't help but notice that his eyes were red-rimmed and bloodshot. He wore the same clothes he'd had on the night before. "You didn't go home at all last night, did you?" she observed.

Shawn shook his head. "I caught a few Zs in my office, though. I wanted to be here early to let in the exterminator. He's already laid traps for the mice and gone. Come to the dining room. I want to show you something."

Shawn came out from behind the bar, and Nancy followed him into the empty dining room. Large, bold, framed posters depicting the Grand Canyon and other desert scenes adorned the wall. "I ran down to Poster Corner in the mall and picked these up when they opened at nine this morning," Shawn said proudly.

"They look great," Nancy said. "What have you done with the slashed paintings?"

"I put them into the storage closet," he replied.

"What will you tell Felice Wainwright?" Nancy asked.

"I don't know." Shawn sighed. "Maybe I'll tell her my customers loved them so much that I sold all seven of them. She'll probably insist I buy more."

Nancy laughed softly. "It's not easy being a business person, is it?"

Shawn shook his head. "And you think Jack has something to do with all this?" he asked.

"I don't know what to think right now," Nancy said honestly. "But I'd like to check him out. Could you give me Jack's phone number and address?"

"They're upstairs in my file," Shawn told her, heading toward his office. "But Jack's not home. I've been calling him all morning. No one picks up the phone."

"Is he scheduled to work today?" Nancy asked.

"Tonight," Shawn said. "We'll have the chance to confront him then."

"If he shows up," Nancy added.

As they reached the hallway, Loreen appeared in the front doorway. "You're here early." Shawn greeted her with a tense smile.

"A little," Loreen said, casting a frosty glance at Nancy. "Why was the back door locked?"

"I want to see who's coming in and out," Shawn told her. "I don't want any more fires or secret additions to the food." Then he excused himself and disappeared up the stairs.

Realizing that this was her chance to talk to Loreen, Nancy stayed behind. Maybe Loreen would reveal something new about the case. Since both intruders had been men, Nancy knew that Loreen hadn't been at the restaurant last night. Still, it wasn't unheard of for a woman to hire someone to work for her. And after Loreen's fit of anger last night, Nancy still considered her a suspect.

Nancy followed the head waitress into the coatroom, where she was hanging up her denim jacket. "Loreen," Nancy said, "we seem to have gotten off to a bad start. I'm not sure why, but I just want to say that—"

"Don't play Little Miss Innocent with me," Loreen snapped. "I know what you're up to."

Nancy took a step back. She had to think fast. What did Loreen know?

"Let me fill you in on one thing," Loreen continued. "Despite what you may have heard, Shawn is taken. He and I are simply having an extended lovers' quarrel, that's all."

Deciding to take a bold approach, Nancy lifted her chin defiantly. "That's not how it looks to me," she said, baiting Loreen. Nancy knew that angry people sometimes revealed things that they might not ordinarily say.

Loreen's pale skin turned a deep crimson. "You don't stand a chance with him!"

"I think Shawn is cute, and he appears to be available," Nancy taunted.

Loreen's emotional temperature dropped from red-hot to an intimidating cool in a matter of seconds. "Listen," she purred, stepping toward Nancy, "everything was fine between Shawn and me until we came here. Then all you flirty River Heights girls started throwing yourselves at Shawn. Between that and all the time this place takes to run, well, it was just too much for any relationship to take."

"Maybe you should go back to Arizona if you hate it here so much," Nancy suggested calmly, hoping to anger Loreen further so she would reveal something.

"Maybe I just will," Loreen replied. "But you can be sure it will be with Shawn. It's only a matter of time before he realizes that this isn't the place for him."

"Oh, here you are, Nancy," Shawn said, coming to the entrance to the coatroom. His blue eyes flashed between Nancy and Loreen. "Is everything okay here?" he asked.

"No problem," Loreen said quickly as she pushed past Nancy and left the coatroom.

Shawn looked at Nancy. "What happened?"

"Loreen wants you back," Nancy answered directly. "She told me to stay away."

Shawn looked sad. "Loreen and I had a great

thing going. Leaving Arizona just seems to have thrown her for a loop."

"It must be hard to make a big move like that," Nancy told him. "Maybe you shouldn't be so tough on Loreen."

"Maybe." Shawn shrugged. "So what's the next step here, Nancy?"

"I think I should discuss those paintings with Felice Wainwright," Nancy answered.

"Good idea," Shawn said. "I have her unlisted number in my office."

"Sorry to send you running up there again," Nancy said. "I'll go with you."

As they climbed the stairs Nancy considered what Loreen had said to her. The head waitress now had two possible motives for wanting to wreck Shawn's business. One was revenge for being dumped. The more likely one, however, was that she wanted Shawn to give up and go back to Arizona with her.

"Here's Jack's address and Felice Wainwright's number," Shawn said when they'd reached his office. "You can use the phone here but please don't tell Mrs. Wainwright what's been going on. I can't risk her canceling the dinner."

"Okay," Nancy agreed. Shawn left, and a moment later Bess appeared in the doorway.

"Hi," she said. "I came in just as you were headed upstairs. What's new?"

"Lots," Nancy said. She filled Bess in on everything that had happened.

"Wow!" Bess exclaimed. "You must be completely exhausted. This case is getting creepier by the minute."

"I know," Nancy agreed as she punched in Felice Wainwright's number. After speaking briefly with the butler, Nancy was connected directly to the heiress.

"Hello," Felice Wainwright answered.

Nancy quickly concocted a story. She said she had seen Joseph Spaziente's work at the Arizona House and was interested in buying a painting. She asked if Felice knew where she could learn more about the artist and his work.

To Nancy's relief, Felice warmed instantly to the subject. Her voice became animated with enthusiasm. "My dear, you have exquisite taste," she said. "I believe Joseph will be a very important painter. He's a genius, really. I happen to have an original Spaziente, which the artist himself has just finished. Would you care to come see it?"

"Absolutely," Nancy said, trying not to sound too eager. "When can I come?"

"Let me see," Felice mused. "I'm attending a dinner party tonight. Can you come now?"

"I'll be there in fifteen minutes," Nancy said.

"Do you need directions?" Felice asked.

"Yes, please," Nancy said, thinking it was unwise to admit that she knew exactly where the woman lived.

"You're going to the Wainwright mansion!" Bess

78

squealed when Nancy hung up. "I don't believe it. Oh, let me come with you, please? I *have* to see it!"

"Don't you have to work?" Nancy asked, laughing.

Bess frowned. "Oh . . . right."

Just then, Shawn came into the office. "I'm heading over to the Wainwright estate," Nancy told him. "I'll be back as soon as I can."

"Can I go with her?" Bess asked. "It's really warm out. No one is going to have a coat today."

"Okay," Shawn said with a laugh. "Go ahead. But remember, not a word about what's been going on. Especially not about the slashed paintings."

In minutes the two girls were heading up the road toward the Wainwright estate. Bess squeezed Nancy's arm as she drove. "This morning, when I woke up, I never dreamed I would be going here. I wish I'd worn a nicer dress. Do I look all right?"

"You look fine, better than I do," Nancy said. She was still wearing the black pants and denim shirt of her waitress uniform.

"Don't worry. The truly rich always dress casually. They don't have to impress anyone," Bess said confidently. "You can say you were out playing polo. You just jumped off your Thoroughbred horse and dashed right over, dah-ling!"

"Good idea," Nancy said, laughing. She reached the estate and pulled into the long drive. The rolling lawn was immaculately groomed. Fruit trees in full pink bloom dotted the landscape, along with squared-off hedges and sculpted azalea bushes bursting with pink and white blossoms.

At the door, the girls were greeted by a tall, stodgy butler. After she gave her name, Nancy and Bess were directed to a large room off the front foyer.

"This place is amazing," Bess whispered, taking in the exquisite antique furnishings and twelve-foot-high ceilings.

"That's by Spaziente, I think," Nancy said, pointing to a painting on the wall. It stood by itself in a gilded frame, just above a long cherry-wood table. "I recognize the style from the paintings in the restaurant."

"The guy is kind of in a rut, don't you think?" Bess said, frowning. "He keeps painting the same thing over and over."

Nancy saw what her friend meant. All of Spaziente's paintings seemed to be landscapes of wooded areas. And this was the third time Nancy had come across this scene, showing the lake in the woods. He'd painted it in summer and in spring. And here it was again. The painting on the wall depicted the same lake and trees, but in autumn, with the woods full of gold and red leaves. Nancy's eye went to the tree in the lower lefthand corner. That tree stood in exactly the spot where the other paintings had been cut. What was so special about that triangle? She reached out to touch it, then drew back her hand as she heard a voice behind her.

"Hello. I'm Felice Wainwright." The wealthy widow seemed to glide into the room. Looking her over, Nancy guessed that Felice was in her early fifties. Her blond hair, swept up in a French twist, crowned her perfect features and light blue eyes. A brocade vest topped a flowing blouse of gossamer silk. Tailored tan pants completed the outfit.

Nancy introduced herself and Bess. "I see you've already spotted Joseph's work," Felice said, nodding toward the painting. "Like van Gogh, Joseph has the ability to imbue his landscapes with the teeming energy of nature."

Bess and Nancy exchanged sidelong glances. It was an attractive painting. But Nancy wasn't sure she'd compare it with a van Gogh. Yet, for the sake of her cover, she had to pretend to be as impressed with the painting as Felice was.

"It is extraordinary," Nancy agreed.

"It's such a shame that Joseph is incarcerated in that awful place," Felice said with a sigh. "I do hope he gets parole soon. Did you know he was once a brilliant electrical engineer? It seems that whatever he touches is marked with his particular genius."

"Why is he in jail?" Bess asked bluntly.

"He shouldn't be, if you ask me," Felice said with a wave of her hand. "He was in debt and got involved with a bank robbery. He was the only one caught. And he didn't hurt anyone."

"Robbing a bank is still a crime," Bess pointed out. Nancy frowned at her.

"Of course, but Joseph's such a gentle soul. He's hardly a menace to society," Felice insisted.

"Would you be willing to sell me this painting?" Nancy asked.

"This painting was a gift from Joseph," Felice replied. "I would part with it, though, if you are really interested."

Just then, a voice boomed from behind them. "That, my good woman, is completely out of the question!" Nancy whirled around and saw a heavy-set, elderly man with wild white hair and wire-rimmed glasses standing imperiously in the doorway. "The painting is mine!"

8

Murky Water

"Who are you, and how did you get in here?" Felice demanded of the man.

"I am Auguste Spaziente," replied the rotund gentleman, stepping into the room.

"I'm so sorry, Mrs. Wainwright," said the butler, rushing into the room. "This—this *person* pushed right past me."

"I will not be dictated to by hired help," the stranger declared as he advanced toward the painting on the wall. "My nephew, Joseph, has informed me that his latest work is hanging in your home, Mrs. Wainwright. I lost not a moment in coming to see it since it does, in fact, belong to me."

Nancy studied the man. Something about him struck her as odd. For someone of his age, who was so heavy, he moved with a jaunty spring in his step. And his hair was so snowy white. Nancy wondered if it was a wig.

He's probably just a spry old bald man who wears a wig, Nancy decided finally.

"Shall I call the police?" the butler asked.

"No, Conrad. It's all right," Felice replied as Auguste planted a kiss on her hand. "How did you know I was Felice Wainwright?" she asked.

"Joseph has described your regal beauty to me many times," he replied.

"Why doesn't he lay it on a little thicker?" Bess whispered to Nancy.

Spaziente looked at Bess sharply. Then his face softened. "Ah," he murmured, "I'm a lucky man to find three beauties clustered in one room."

"This is Bess Marvin and Nancy Drew," Felice said. "Now, how may I help you?"

"It seems I came here just in time," Spaziente said. "You were about to sell something that rightfully belongs to me."

"To you?" Nancy questioned.

"Indeed. My nephew told me that he left a painting for me with Mrs. Wainwright. He said I should come here to collect it. I own a gallery back in New York, you see. I am in the perfect position to give Joseph the showing his art so richly deserves."

"There must be some mistake," Felice insisted. "Joseph gave this to me as a gift. I was only willing to part with it so that Joseph could have as wide an audience as possible."

"All the more reason to give *me* the painting," Auguste said. "Though the rest of the Spaziente family has abandoned Joseph—they feel disgraced

84

by his brush with the law—I am standing by him. I believe in his genius, and I am just the person to give him a new start."

Felice sighed. "I was about to tell Nancy, and now I'll tell you both. I'm not parting with the painting until after this weekend. You may have heard about the auction I'm holding on Saturday. Collectors from all over the world will be here in this room. I want them to see Joseph's work. Seven of his paintings are hanging at the Arizona House, where I'll be holding a preauction dinner party. Then, when everyone comes back here, they'll see this one, Joseph's finest. It's just the kind of exposure he needs. I can't take this painting out of the collection now."

Inwardly, Nancy cringed. What would happen when Felice discovered the other paintings had been destroyed? She wouldn't be too pleased, that was for sure.

"But Joseph has promised this painting to me," Spaziente protested. "I must have it now."

Nancy's eyes narrowed slightly as she gazed at the man. Did he really want to put the painting in his gallery? Or was he trying to get his hands on the painting for the same reason the intruder in the restaurant had slashed Spaziente's other paintings?

"I'll see Joseph in art class on Friday," Felice said. "He can decide the fate of this painting. Is that fair enough?"

A look of annoyance crossed Auguste's face, but he seemed to hold back his irritation. "How can I refuse such a lovely lady? In the interest of fairness, I will wait two more days."

"Thank you, Mr. Spaziente," Felice said.

"You are quite welcome," he replied, bowing slightly. "I will show myself to the door. It was a pleasure to meet you ladies."

Bowing again to them all, he turned and left.

"What a character," Bess said when he was gone.

"Charming, though," Felice said thoughtfully.

Nancy couldn't help but feel that Auguste Spaziente was not on the level. Was he working with Joseph Spaziente? Or perhaps the man was an imposter. Maybe Joseph Spaziente didn't even know he existed. "Has Joseph ever mentioned his uncle to you before?" she asked.

Felice shook her head. "No, but Joseph is not a talkative man."

"Shawn told me about your art program for prisoners," Nancy said. "Would you say it's been a success?"

"Undoubtedly," Felice replied without hesitation. "So many of these men have untapped talent. It gives them a way to harness their creative energies constructively."

"It's a great idea," Nancy said sincerely.

Felice's eyes brightened. "Would you like to come to Friday's class? It would give you the opportunity to meet Joseph. Rather than buy an existing painting, perhaps you could commission a work from him."

"That would be wonderful," Nancy said. It was a

great opportunity. She had a feeling that Joseph Spaziente was the key to whatever was going on here. Meeting him might give her some idea of where he fit in.

"Would you like to come, too, Bess?" Felice asked.

"I would, but I have to work," Bess said.

Felice turned to Nancy. "The prisoners are taken by bus to the River Heights Community Center. They're all nonviolent offenders, but still, the security is rather tight," Felice told her. "I'll have to call and get you a security pass. But since today is Wednesday, I'll have two days to get the paperwork done. I don't think it will be a problem." Felice ripped a piece of paper from a notepad on a table. "Write your name, address, and social security number here."

"What time is the class?" Nancy asked as she wrote.

"Meet me at the front door of the Center at eleven," Felice instructed her. "Now, ladies, you must excuse me. I'm due to meet a friend for lunch."

Felice walked Bess and Nancy to the front door. "See you soon," she said, shutting the door.

"What a classy lady," Bess commented. "What did you think of Uncle Auguste?"

"There was definitely something odd about him," Nancy replied. "I felt as if I'd seen him before."

"Nan, I think you'd remember if you'd met him

before," Bess said. "He wasn't exactly your average guy on the street."

"That's true," Nancy agreed with a chuckle. "I wonder if I've seen him on the news."

"So how do you think all this fits together?" Bess asked.

"I don't know," Nancy admitted. "But somehow, I think the problems at the restaurant are related to Joseph Spaziente's paintings. I hope meeting him will shed some light on that."

Bess looked at her watch. It was noon. "We'd better get back to work," she said.

Nancy nodded. "I want to see what's going on back at the restaurant."

When Nancy and Bess arrived at the Arizona House, the parking lot was full. Nancy parked behind the building, and they entered the restaurant through the back entrance.

"Look," Bess said, grabbing Nancy's arm as soon as they walked out of the kitchen. "Harold Brackett is back. He's giving the restaurant another chance, just as he promised."

Nancy saw the food critic enter the dining room behind Lee, the maître d'. As she watched, Shawn came up beside her.

"I'm glad you got back in time," he said. "I want you to serve Harold Brackett. Do you think you're up to it?"

"I haven't really waited on a table yet," Nancy reminded him.

"I know, but you're the only one I can trust. If

anything else goes wrong, I'm finished. I can't afford to get a bad review. I'll guide you through it, and I won't give you any other customers."

"I'll give it a shot," Nancy said gamely.

"What's going on?" Loreen asked, stopping on her way to the lounge.

"I'm letting Nancy try her hand at waiting on a table. She'll wait on Harold Brackett," Shawn responded firmly.

"Isn't she kind of inexperienced?" Loreen pointed out.

"I have my reasons, Loreen," Shawn said levelly.

"You're the boss," Loreen said with a shrug as she continued on her way.

Turning back to Nancy, Shawn placed one hand on her shoulder and walked her into the dining room. "Just give him a menu and ask if he'd like a drink to start."

"Got it," Nancy said, picking a menu out of a wooden holder on the wall.

Harold Brackett's eyes flickered with recognition when Nancy approached his table. "Don't I know you from somewhere?" he asked.

"I was here the other day when you got the, uh, hot fish," she said, regretting that she had to remind him of the incident.

"Ah, yes . . . the fish," Brackett said with an ironic smile. "What would you recommend I try this time?"

Nancy suggested he try the seafood burrito that her father had liked. She asked if he wanted a drink, and the critic ordered a glass of white wine. "Your best Chardonnay, please," he said.

"Coming right up," Nancy said.

While Brackett studied the menu, Nancy went to the lounge for his drink. "We usually only sell this stuff by the bottle," Roy said as he popped the cork of the wine bottle. "But for Mr. Harold Brackett, we'll open our best Chardonnay and pour one glass."

"Thanks," Nancy said as he handed her the glass of wine. It wobbled on the small round cocktail tray. "Whoa!" she said. "Balancing a drink isn't as easy as it looks."

"Hold the tray underneath and hold the glass stem with your other hand," Roy told her. "After a while you'll be able to do it with one hand. It just takes practice."

With her eyes trained on the glass, Nancy slowly made her way into the dining room. From the corner of her eye, she noticed Loreen efficiently balancing a large tray stacked high with lunches, glasses, and a water pitcher. Loreen was moving rapidly in her direction.

As Nancy neared Brackett's table, she side-stepped slightly to veer out of Loreen's path. "Here you go, Mr. Brackett," she began as she gingerly lifted the glass from the tray.

Suddenly, as Loreen passed by, Nancy felt the waitress's foot hook sharply around her ankle.

Oooph! Nancy pitched forward. As if in slow

motion, she watched the wine spray in every direction as she fell to the floor.

A hush descended over the dining room as all eyes turned toward Nancy. I don't believe this, she thought, mortified. Miraculously, when she looked at Brackett, she saw he was untouched by the wine. Most of it had splashed onto the wall.

To Nancy's surprise, Brackett jumped to his feet to help her up. Loreen had put her tray down on an empty table nearby. "Clumsy, clumsy," she said.

Nancy glared at her.

"Give this young woman some water," Brackett told Loreen. He picked a glass off Loreen's tray and held it while Loreen filled it. Then he turned away from Nancy and Loreen, still holding the glass.

"What's the matter?" Loreen asked the man.

"I thought I detected a chip in this glass," Brackett said, turning to the girls. "I wanted to see it better."

"Let me see," Loreen said, taking the glass from him. She walked away a few paces and held it to a ray of sunlight coming in from the skylight. "I don't see any chip," she said with a shrug.

"Perhaps it was just a reflection," Brackett said as he handed Nancy the glass.

A throbbing knot was beginning to form on Nancy's forehead. "Thanks," she said to Brackett as she sipped the water. "I'm so sorry."

Brackett sniffed. "This restaurant does seem to be the center of all calamities in the western hemisphere. But I'm sure it's not your fault. Tell me, what should I expect next? An earthquake? A tidal wave?"

Despite her embarrassment, Nancy laughed.

"The only disaster around here is *you*," Loreen snapped. She glared at Nancy, then picked up her tray and walked off.

Brackett raised his eyebrows. "A fan?"

"Not exactly," Nancy said. "In fact, she tripped me."

"I suspected that was the case," Brackett sympathized. "Tell me, Nancy Drew, what disasters befell the paintings on the wall?"

Nancy decided not to tell Brackett the truth. He didn't need to know that the restaurant was under siege. "Shawn thought the Southwestern scenes would be more in keeping with the rest of the decor," she said truthfully.

"I see. Shawn doesn't plan to display any more original artwork?" Brackett asked.

"He might," Nancy replied, remembering Shawn telling her Felice would probably want him to buy more paintings. "Why do you ask?"

"Atmosphere is part of a restaurant's total picture," the critic replied. "I consider food, service, and ambiance in my reviews."

"Well, let's get the service part back on track," Nancy said. "Do you know what you'd like to order?"

"I'll try the seafood burrito, as you suggested,"

Brackett told her. "And I will begin with the fried oysters."

"I'll place your order, then I'll be back with another drink," Nancy said, turning away from the table. She headed across the restaurant to the kitchen door.

"How's it going?" Shawn asked anxiously.

"All right," she said, reading him Brackett's order. She decided not to tell him that Loreen had tripped her. He had enough to worry about.

When Nancy went out to the lounge, she said to Roy, "Good thing you opened that bottle. I need another glass of wine."

"Yeah, one of the waitresses told me what happened," Roy said kindly as he poured the glass. "That Loreen has really got it out for you."

"I guess," Nancy said, taking the glass from him. She looked at the wine sloshing in the glass and realized her hand was shaking.

"Hey, kid, relax," Roy said, taking back the glass. "Don't let what happened get to you."

"It's not that. I feel a little strange all of a sudden," Nancy said. She felt weak, and her mouth was dry.

"Did you hurt yourself when you fell?" Roy asked.

The shakiness passed slightly, and Nancy felt better. "I'll be okay," she said, heading back into the dining room with the glass of wine.

After delivering his drink, Nancy served Brackett

the fried oysters, which he seemed to like. When his lunch was ready to serve, she carefully loaded it onto her tray.

But as she crossed the dining room, concentrating on balancing her tray, her legs felt like lead. Everything around her suddenly seemed elongated and wavy. The noises of the restaurant had become garbled, as though she was listening to them from underwater.

Suddenly the room spun madly. Nancy was aware of her tray clattering to the floor. Then the wavering shapes before her eyes melted into total blackness.

9

Newsworthy Clues

Tick . . . tick . . . tick . . . Nancy was vaguely aware of the steady, gentle sound. She opened her eyes into a hazy cloud. Slowly, the cloud cleared, and Nancy sat up, propping herself on her elbows.

She was in a hospital room. The sound was coming from a monitor hooked to the sleeping woman in the next bed. Rays of a golden sunset fell through the blinds, forming lines on Nancy's blanket.

Carson Drew appeared in the doorway, accompanied by a doctor in a white lab coat. "How are you feeling, Nan?" her father asked.

"I don't know." Nancy blinked. Her head ached, and she felt weak. "What happened?" she asked.

"You've been sleeping, probably because of the drug we found in your system," the handsome, dark-haired doctor explained. "I'm Dr. Russo. Your father told me the kind of work you do, so on a hunch we ran a blood test. It came up positive for Seconal. That's a water-soluble, short-term barbiturate. Do you remember the last thing you drank before you passed out?"

"A glass of water," Nancy said, gingerly pressing the bandage that covered her forearm, where they'd taken blood.

"Anything before that?" Dr. Russo asked.

Nancy shook her head. "Just a glass of orange juice at breakfast, around ten."

"Then it was the water," Dr. Russo said. "Where did you get it from?"

"It was in a pitcher at the restaurant," Nancy replied.

"Do you know who drugged you?" her father asked.

Nancy thought for a minute. Both Brackett and Loreen had been nearby when she drank the water. But why would Brackett drug her? It had to have been Loreen. Unless the drugged water had been in the pitcher and was meant for a customer— another act of sabotage. Maybe it had even been meant for Brackett himself. After all, he'd been the target of an earlier mishap. "I'm not really sure who did it," Nancy answered finally.

"Whoever did it didn't want you out of commission for long," the doctor said. "Seconal is fast-acting, but short-term. It was probably done to scare you more than to hurt you. You'll be fine. I'm going to sign you out of the hospital, but I want you to go straight home and get into bed."

"Thanks for everything, Doctor," Carson said, shaking Dr. Russo's hand.

When the doctor was gone, Nancy's father sat on the edge of her bed. "Is there anything I can say to convince you to drop this case?" he asked.

Nancy leaned forward, letting her red-blond hair fall over her shoulders. "I don't think so, Dad."

"I was afraid of that," he said, putting his arm around her and helping her up from the hospital bed. "Let's go home."

That night, Nancy fell into a dark, dreamless sleep. She awoke Thursday morning feeling rubber-limbed but generally restored. The thought of spending the entire day in bed made her instantly restless. Besides, she had only two days left before Shawn's important dinner on Saturday. She had to have this case solved by then!

After showering and dressing, Nancy went downstairs. Her father had already left for work. She was just finishing breakfast when the doorbell rang. It was Bess.

"How are you feeling?" she asked, coming into the hallway.

"Better, thanks," Nancy said, closing the door. "Someone drugged me."

"I know," Bess said. "Your father told me when I called last night." She frowned. "I bet it was Loreen. Oh, Nancy, this case is getting too dangerous."

"What happened after I passed out?" Nancy asked.

Bess rolled her eyes. "It was crazy. I called an ambulance and then your father right away. In the middle of all that, Shawn and Loreen had this huge fight. One of the other waitresses, I think it was Anne Marie, had seen Loreen trip you, and she told Shawn. He was furious. He actually fired Loreen!"

"Wow," Nancy said, shaking her head. "Did Jack ever show up for work?"

"Nope. Never showed."

Nancy curled up on the living room couch, and Bess settled in beside her.

"What about Brackett?" Nancy asked.

"He stormed out, muttering something about unbelievable incompetence," Bess said. "No one knows if he'll be back or not."

"Shawn must be tearing his hair out," Nancy said.

Bess fished in her purse and pulled out a small card with an address written on it. "I did a little detective work of my own," she said, handing the card to Nancy. "I filched this from Shawn's file."

It was Loreen's address. Nancy recognized the location. It was an apartment building in downtown River Heights. "I figured you might need it," Bess added.

"Thanks," Nancy said, bending the card gently between her fingers. "I need to check her out a little more—especially since she might be the person who slipped that knockout drug in my water."

Nancy got to her feet and stretched. "But first, I

need to brush up on the recent history of River Heights."

"Sure, but why?" Bess replied.

"Because, frankly, I'm stumped," Nancy admitted. "I have a lot of pieces here, but they just don't fit together. Jack hasn't been back to the restaurant, yet someone drugged me. So I know he's not working alone. He might be in cahoots with Loreen. But then, who was the other man I saw slicing the paintings? And how do Felice, the paintings, and Joe Spaziente fit in? I can't make the connections. I'd like to look through back issues of the newspaper and see what I can learn about Felice Wainwright and her charity events."

When the girls arrived at the River Heights public library, they went straight to the periodical room. Nancy asked the librarian for back issues and microfilm of several River Heights papers. Then she settled in on a comfortable chair to sort through them.

Over at the magazine rack, Bess selected two on food and three on fashion. "This is my kind of investigating," she said, cracking a piece of bubble gum.

Nancy found several articles that interested her. One was a report on Felice's purchase of the Dragon's Eye Ruby. It said that Felice, a personal friend of actor Gary Powell, had quietly purchased the giant stone from Powell. It went on to tell how the Dragon's Eye Ruby was the largest of its kind in the world. The gem had an interesting history, having been the property of several Chinese emperors before being smuggled out of the country during a period of political turmoil.

Skimming the papers, Nancy found an article published six months later in which Felice announced her intention to sell the ruby. "There are so many worthy causes that would benefit from the money," she told the paper. "It seems absurd for me to have it locked in a vault. But because the money will go to charity, I will insist on receiving the highest price possible. This is an international event. The ruby will attract interested parties from all over the world."

As she flipped through the pages, Nancy's eye was drawn to an article on the opening of the Arizona House. It showed Shawn and Loreen, arm in arm, standing in front of the restaurant. Gazing fondly at each other, they seemed very much in love.

Paging through a paper from the previous week, Nancy spotted another brief article on Felice Wainwright. It described how Mrs. Wainwright's security system had been tripped, setting off lights and alarms and immediately summoning the private security guard who had a direct line to the system. No intruder was found, and nothing was taken. "This system is obviously one hundred percent effective," the head of the security force was quoted as saying.

Nancy put the papers aside and went to the

microfilm machine. Reduced on film were many back issues of the *River Heights Review*. Snapping in the cartridge, she began scanning the articles.

She stopped when a familiar name jumped out at her: Joseph Spaziente. His name was printed below a picture of a sharp-featured man with dark, scowling eyes and lightly pockmarked skin. The article reported that only one burglar, Spaziente, had been caught during the midnight break-in of a local bank. He'd been shot in the leg while holding open the back door of the getaway van for the other escaping criminals. He fell to the ground while the van sped off without him.

The article went on to say that authorities still could not figure out how the thieves had short-circuited the bank's security system. The alarm never sounded, and they managed to get through elaborate locks. If a passing patrol car hadn't noticed activity at the back of the bank, the thieves would have gotten away with a perfect crime. As it turned out, Spaziente had been holding the suitcase of money, and it tumbled to the ground with him when he was shot.

When she finished the article, Nancy took out the cartridge and gave her materials back to the librarian. "Ready to go?" she asked Bess, who sat engrossed in an issue of *Fine Food* magazine.

"Look what I found," she said, showing Nancy the article. "It's a review by Harold Brackett."

"'Summer's finest foods,'" Nancy read aloud.

" 'When I was a ten-year-old boy in Brooklyn, my brother took me on the Parachute Jump ride at Coney Island. Afterward,' " she continued reading, " 'we went for a frankfurter with mustard and sauerkraut. For years that frankfurter embodied all that was wonderful about summer. But through the years I cultivated more sophisticated tastes . . .' "

Nancy looked up from the article and stared into space thoughtfully.

"What's the matter, Nan?" Bess asked.

"Nothing," Nancy replied. "I was just thinking of something. The Harold Brackett we saw at the restaurant is only in his early thirties. He isn't old enough to have been on the Parachute Jump when he was ten. The ride was closed down before then."

"Maybe he just made the whole thing up because it sounded good," Bess suggested.

"Mmmm," Nancy mused. "Maybe. Or maybe the guy we know isn't really Harold Brackett." Nancy handed the magazine back to Bess. "Come on. I want to snoop around Loreen's neighborhood a little. It's not far from here. We can talk to her neighbors and find out if Jack has come around to see her. If she's there, I want to talk to her directly."

Ten minutes later, Nancy and Bess arrived at the apartment complex. They buzzed Loreen's bell, but no one answered on the intercom. "Good," said Nancy, motioning Bess inside. "She's not home."

"What exactly are we trying to do?" Bess asked as

the girls rode the elevator up to the eleventh floor.

"I'm going to try to talk to some of Loreen's neighbors," Nancy said. "Maybe I can learn something that way. I'll say I'm a cousin who's looking for her."

The elevator reached their floor, and the girls got out. Suddenly Bess stepped back into the elevator and pulled Nancy with her.

"What's wrong?" Nancy asked.

"Apartment Eleven C. That's Loreen's, and the door is open," Bess whispered.

Nancy held the elevator door open while she considered her next move. "Let's go check it out. If she's home, I'll think of some reason for us to be here. I'll say I want to be friends or something like that."

"Oh, I'm sure she'd really love that," Bess said, reluctantly following Nancy into the hall.

Cautiously, Nancy pushed open the door. "Hello," she called in.

Bess peeked in behind Nancy and gasped. There was a man inside the apartment! He was coming out of a doorway off the narrow front hall. He was dressed in coveralls and held a toolbox.

"Sorry to scare you," he told the girls. "Your sink is fixed. I'll give the spare key to the super on the way out."

"Great. Thanks a lot," Nancy said, closing the door behind the plumber.

"What a lucky break," Bess commented.

"I'll say," Nancy agreed. "Bess, you keep an eye

out through the peephole on the door. I want to do some snooping."

Loreen's apartment was small and neat. Nancy found mail scattered on one table. She read through an opened phone bill on the top. Loreen's long-distance bill totaled over a hundred dollars. Most of the calls were to Arizona.

Next Nancy played Loreen's phone answering machine. One call was from her mother. The second call was more interesting.

"Loreen, this is Edward from Le St. Tropez. Please call me."

Nancy pressed the Save button, and the tape rewound. Loreen would never know anyone else had heard her messages.

Perching on the arm of a beige loveseat, Nancy thought about this latest clue. Was Loreen helping Le St. Tropez sabotage their competition, the Arizona House? Was she doing it to get back at Shawn for breaking their engagement? For money? Or was she simply looking for another job? And how did the paintings figure into the equation? They didn't. Not yet, anyway.

"Nancy! Loreen's coming!" Bess whispered urgently.

Nancy jumped up and looked around. "The fire escape," she told Bess. "Hurry!"

Nancy and Bess opened the back window, which adjoined the fire escape, and slipped out.

"Climb down," Nancy urged Bess.

Bess moaned. "This makes me very nervous."

"Bess, just get to the next floor so she doesn't see us," Nancy said.

Casting a worried glance over her shoulder, Bess lowered herself down the metal ladder. Just as Nancy was about to follow, Loreen came through the door. Nancy plastered herself to the brick wall of the building. She waited a few moments, then peeked in through the window. She was in time to see the back of Loreen's leg as she stepped into the bathroom. Nancy hurried down the fire escape and joined Bess on the lower landing.

"It's a long way down," Bess fretted.

"Hang on tight and keep going," Nancy said.

After a long climb, Nancy and Bess reached the bottom landing.

"How do I let you talk me into these things?" Bess said as she hung from the drop bar at the bottom of the escape.

Nancy had already jumped to the ground. She yanked down the bottom ladder so that Bess was able to climb all the way to the pavement.

"See? That wasn't so bad," Nancy said, brushing herself off as they made their way back to her car.

"Right. What's eleven floors of sheer terror? Nothing!" Bess said dryly.

Nancy dropped Bess off at her house, then headed home. For once, she was glad her father's car wasn't in the driveway. He wouldn't be happy if he knew she hadn't been in bed all day.

When Nancy pushed open the front door, she immediately spotted a long white envelope lying on the front hall carpet. It looked as if someone had slipped it under the door.

Nancy picked up the envelope and tore it open. It took only a second to read. The note read, "Give up, Nancy Drew—while you still can."

10

Relative Danger

For the next hour, Nancy read and reread the note. She didn't show it to her father when he came home, thinking he was already worried enough.

Though the words were printed, some of the letters drifted into script. The *i* was very distinctive, curving far back like an inverted *c*. The points of the final *n* in "can" were also sharp and decisive. The paper was good-quality bond with a grain. The rough edges at the top told Nancy it had been torn from a pad. She tried to decide whether it was written by a male or female hand, but it was hard to tell.

Nancy sighed. She'd been threatened before, on other cases. But this person, she knew, wasn't kidding around. How far would he or she go?

The next morning Nancy dressed in black pants and a soft blue silk blouse. She pulled her hair back with a blue barrette. After breakfast, she drove to the River Heights Community Center. Felice Wainwright was waiting for her.

"Here's your pass," Felice said, handing Nancy a large white card. "The class is just down this hall."

"Do you enjoy teaching?" Nancy asked as they walked down the long, quiet corridor.

"Oh, yes. Mostly I do a lot of encouraging. I studied art in Rome for a number of years, so I can give the men a few pointers and principles, too."

They stopped at a door in front of which stood two uniformed guards. "She's with me," Felice said as Nancy held up her pass.

Inside the bright, high-ceilinged room, ten men dressed in gray coveralls worked intently on canvases propped on easels. In each corner of the room stood armed guards.

The prisoners looked up from their work when Nancy and Felice entered. Taking Nancy's arm, Felice guided her over to a short, dark-haired man working in oils. Nancy immediately recognized Joseph Spaziente from his picture in the paper.

"Joseph, this is Nancy Drew. She's a great fan of your work. She might be interested in commissioning a piece," Felice said.

Spaziente looked up at Nancy, then turned back to his work. "I don't do commissions," he muttered as he dabbed his brush in the paint on his palette.

The scene Spaziente worked on had already been sketched in pencil on the canvas. Nancy noticed that the subject was the same as the other three she'd seen, a lake surrounded by trees. The sketch was done in light lines with little detail—except for the tree in the lower left-hand corner. Every inch of its bark had been penciled in with great care.

"That lake scene seems to captivate you," Nancy said pleasantly.

"Mmmph," he grunted in reply. With one long, decisive stroke, he covered the sketch marks on the tree trunk with a long line of brown paint.

"Once you've completed this winter scene, the series will be finished," Felice said. "Spring and summer are in the Arizona House. I have autumn. Where shall we send winter?"

The dull boredom in Spaziente's eyes was replaced with sharp interest. "Hasn't my Uncle Auguste been in touch with you?"

"I was just about to mention that," Felice said, slightly flustered. "He says you promised him the painting you gave to me."

"I'll paint you another," Spaziente said gruffly. "Give him the painting. I want him to have this one, too."

Felice's mouth twitched. The gift had obviously meant something to her.

"But, Joseph," Felice protested, "can't your uncle wait until after my auction? So many important people will see your work and—"

"I want Auguste to have the paintings!" Spaziente flared. Red-faced with anger, he jumped up from his seat.

Startled, Felice backed up clumsily, upsetting a

small table on which Spaziente had piled art books and sketches.

In a flash, two guards closed in on Spaziente. Taking him by either arm, they wordlessly ushered him out of the room.

Felice paled. "Oh, dear! This is awful. The warden is very strict about security. Joseph might be dropped from the program."

"It's not your fault," Nancy said gently.

"It is," Felice insisted. "Joseph has an artistic temperament. I shouldn't have provoked him. He's usually so mild-mannered. I have to explain to the guards." She rushed from the room.

An awkward moment followed. Every prisoner in the room was staring at Nancy. "Back to your work!" snapped one of the guards.

Nancy righted the knocked-over table and stooped to gather the books and sketches that had fallen to the floor. Now that she'd met Spaziente, she saw that he was not the gentle soul Felice believed him to be. The whereabouts of his paintings seemed to mean a lot to him. Nancy wondered if the paintings were connected to the bungled bank robbery—or even to the auction of the Dragon's Eye Ruby.

Suddenly Nancy remembered what the newspaper article had said. Spaziente's gang had disengaged an elaborate security system. Felice also had a complex system. Was there a connection?

As she picked up a heavy book on oil painting,

two pieces of paper slipped out from between its covers. Still bending down, Nancy examined them. One paper was a drawing—a series of lines that ran straight for a while, then zigzagged at uneven intervals. In a small, tight script, Spaziente had written: "final quadrant, winter."

The other was a note that said: "Joe. What's taking so long? Must see your latest work. Where is it going to end up? Everything set. You won't be sorry. Your loving uncle."

Uncle Auguste, no doubt. Nancy stared at the letter. Suddenly, her blood ran cold. The i's bent way back, like inverted c's. The n's were sharp.

Uncle Auguste was the person who had left her the threatening note!

She turned the letter in her hand. It was even written on the same kind of paper, a heavy bond with a slight grain running through it.

Why would August Spaziente threaten her? How did he even know of her connection with the Arizona House case? Had he been the man who slashed the paintings? No. That man hadn't been fat. What did all of this mean?

At that moment, Felice and Joseph returned. Nancy stuffed the papers back into the book and returned them to the table. "Is everything all right?" she asked, rising to her feet.

"Yes. I explained that it was all my fault," Felice said quickly. "You're absolutely right, Joseph. You should do whatever you please with your own paintings. I'll give your uncle the autumn scene, and I'll see that he gets the winter scene as soon as it's completed."

"It'll be done by the end of class," Spaziente said.

"So quickly?" Felice said in surprise.

Spaziente snorted. "I've painted it enough times." He frowned at Nancy. "Get her away from me, would you? I can't work with her breathing over my shoulder."

Felice looked at Nancy apologetically.

"No problem," Nancy said quickly. She'd seen enough, anyway.

She walked down the wide steps of the Community Center and drove off in her car. A few minutes later, she stopped at a phone booth and called Shawn at the Arizona House. He told her Jack hadn't shown up and couldn't be contacted by phone. Nancy decided to drive by Jack's house. She still had his address in her purse.

It wasn't long before she came to a residential part of town. The streets were quiet as she drove past modest homes with small front yards. She parked at the curb in front of Jack's house. It was a one-story, neat house with blue siding. Nancy walked up the path and rang the doorbell. She'd decided to confront Jack directly. She wanted to know exactly what he had against Shawn. And she had to find out if Jack had a partner. Was he working with Loreen? Uncle Auguste? The mysterious intruder? All of them?

As she waited, she noticed that there was no car in the driveway. No one answered the door. Nancy walked around to the back porch and looked into the empty kitchen. The window nearest the door was slightly open. There was no sense waiting around for Jack. It would be a good time to do some investigating on her own.

It wasn't hard for her to raise the screen, reach in, and unlatch the back door. In the next minute, she was standing inside Jack's small kitchen.

The adjoining room was a dining area. The walls were adorned with old photos: the old Chez Jacques, photos of Jack receiving culinary awards, and autographed pictures of Jack with politicians, celebrities, and sports figures. The restaurant had obviously been the center of Jack's life.

As Nancy studied the photos, a sudden noise on the back porch made her jump. She whirled around and saw Jack coming in the door.

"You!" he cried, storming into the dining room. "What are you doing in my house?"

"Looking for you," Nancy said boldly. "I have some questions to ask you."

Jack crossed to the phone on his kitchen wall. "I'm calling the police," he threatened.

"Good!" Nancy called his bluff. "You can tell them why you tried to burn the Arizona House to the ground. You doused the linens with vodka, then threw on a match. It wasn't only arson. It was attempted murder. Bess and I were trapped in that kitchen."

Jack froze. "No," he said, horrified. "Never murder. I didn't mean to hurt anyone." He dropped the phone receiver and sank into a chair. "I simply wanted the kitchen damaged and the restaurant closed for repair. I never meant for anyone to be hurt. Why do you think I let you out of that refrigerator? I am not a cruel man. I only wanted my restaurant back. That kid has no right to that business."

"What do you mean?" Nancy asked.

"His father was a thief!" Jack cried, pounding the arm of the chair angrily. "He took care of the business side. I ran the restaurant and did the cooking. But when he died, I had to take over our accounts. That's when I saw what had been going on. He'd been stealing from our business! Thousands and thousands of dollars had been paid to ABC Beverages. There was no ABC Beverages! It was his own account! The half of the restaurant Shawn Morgan inherited wouldn't even begin to pay me back for all the money his father stole. He'd left no funds in reserve. I couldn't run the place properly with the money that was left. All my creditors wanted to be paid, and there was nothing to pay them with."

"Did you tell this to Shawn?" Nancy asked.

Jack waved his hand in disgust. "Ahh! What good would it have done? Like father, like son. No. I only wanted my restaurant back."

"So you decided to drive Shawn out of business,"

Nancy guessed. "Then what were you planning to do?"

"Buy it back from him, of course," Jack replied. "I recently came into a small inheritance. It's not enough to open a new place of my own. But it's enough to buy a failing restaurant and return it to its former glory. I'll win over all the customers who now dine at Le St. Tropez."

Le St. Tropez. Nancy remembered the message on Loreen's machine. From his words, Nancy deduced that Jack was not working for Shawn's competition. "Are you working with anyone else?" she asked.

Jack looked surprised. "No."

"You're lying," Nancy challenged. "Who slashed the paintings on the wall?"

"The paintings?" Jack asked, confused. "I never touched any paintings."

"Loreen is helping you, isn't she?" Nancy pressed. "She's the one who drugged me."

"Loreen *drugged* you?" Jack asked incredulously.

Nancy's frustration rose. "Jack! Tell me who is working with you. I know for sure that Auguste Spaziente is your partner."

"I have no idea what you're talking about," Jack insisted. Something in his tone convinced Nancy that he was being truthful. "Young lady, I am responsible for a number of mishaps at the restaurant. The *wasabi*, the plumbing, the fire, the mice, the reservation book—yes. But I slashed no paintings, I know no Auguste, and I have nothing to do with drugs. I have not returned to the restaurant since the night you chased me from the kitchen."

"Why not?" Nancy asked.

Jack shrugged. "What was the point? I figured you found me out. I thought I was done for. I have been expecting the police to arrive at any moment."

"Shawn didn't turn you in," Nancy told him.

"Hmmm," Jack said, folding his arms. "And why is that?"

"Because he couldn't believe you would really do such a thing. And because he likes you," Nancy told him.

"Perhaps I misjudged the kid," Jack admitted.

"It seems he misjudged you, too," Nancy said. "Shawn thought you were on his side."

Jack's expression told Nancy her words had stung. "I'll walk you to the door," he said.

"Thanks, but I can find it myself," Nancy said, passing him as she went out the kitchen door.

Nancy drove directly to the Arizona House. She wanted to talk to Shawn. Maybe, between the two of them, they could put the pieces of this mystery together.

When Nancy arrived, the lunch hour was just winding down. "Hi," Lee greeted her in the foyer. "How are you feeling?"

"A lot better," she said. "Is Shawn here?"

"Upstairs," Lee told her.

Nancy found Shawn in his office, poring over his

116

accounts. "Bad news?" she asked, reading his grim expression.

"Pretty bad," he confirmed. "Somehow I have to hang on until after the Wainwright dinner tomorrow night. Once Mrs. Wainwright pays me for that, I can pay off some of this debt that's swamping me."

Nancy was about to speak when Shawn jumped to his feet. "Oh, hello," he said to someone behind Nancy.

Nancy turned and saw Felice Wainwright standing in the office doorway, looking deeply distressed. "Mr. Morgan," she said. "Tomorrow night's dinner is off!"

11

A Change of Plan

Felice suddenly noticed Nancy. "Why, hello, Nancy. What are you doing here?"

"Booking her engagement party," Shawn said before Nancy could open her mouth. "No problem, Nancy. We can accommodate two hundred people."

Nancy didn't contradict him. Shawn was obviously trying to appear confident in the face of this new crisis.

"Now, Mrs. Wainwright, why the sudden cancellation?" Shawn asked.

"I've been hearing most unsettling things about your restaurant, Mr. Morgan. My friend, Dr. Elizabeth Hordell, told me a man was given overspiced fish last Tuesday. I also read in the paper that the fire department was called in recently. I'm truly sorry, but—"

118

"We're having a little trouble with our electrical work," Shawn told Felice. "It caused a tiny little fire, but it's all been fixed. And the fish . . . yes, that was unfortunate. The customer ordered it that way. He fancied himself able to eat the hottest foods. He learned the hard way, I'm afraid." Shawn spoke rapidly.

To Nancy he seemed very nervous, but Felice seemed to be satisfied with the explanations. She relaxed a bit. "And what has happened to my paintings?" Felice asked.

"The paintings . . ." Shawn stalled. "Oh, I'm having them framed. The posters you see in the dining room are just temporary until I get Mr. Spaziente's paintings back."

Felice hesitated. "I suppose that would explain everything, but still—"

"I've just had a great idea," Shawn cut her off. "Why don't we bring the dinner to your house? We can set up tents and tables on your lawn. I'll take care of every detail."

"That *would* be convenient," Felice agreed slowly. "And I suppose it would be difficult to find another location at this late date."

"I knew you'd like the idea," Shawn said, flashing a dazzling smile at Felice. "We'll be set up and ready to go by seven tomorrow."

"The auction starts at nine," Felice reminded him. "There can be no delay. My private security police will close off the entrances and move the ruby downstairs at nine sharp."

119

"Everything will run like clockwork," Shawn assured her.

"I hope so." Felice sighed. "I did want everyone to see Joseph's paintings, though. Do you think I could borrow the ones you have? Just for the evening?"

"Oh, Mrs. Wainwright, I am so sorry," Shawn said. "I sent them to a special framer in Chicago. He's closed through the weekend."

"You sent all seven?" When Shawn nodded, Felice frowned. "Well, I still have the two at my home," she said. "Joseph gave me the winter scene, which he completed this morning."

"Has Auguste Spaziente asked for them yet?" Nancy asked.

Felice squared her shoulders. "As a matter of fact, he was waiting at my home when I returned from the Community Center. I refused to give him the paintings."

"But I thought you agreed to give them to him," Nancy said.

Felice looked embarrassed. "I'm afraid I changed my mind. That man can wait twelve hours for the paintings. This could be a big breakthrough for Joseph. He's let his uncle pressure him into parting with his paintings just when he's on the verge of being discovered."

"Joseph Spaziente doesn't seem like a man who's easily pressured," Nancy said skeptically.

"That Auguste could pressure anyone," Felice

120

said. "He was much less charming today. I detest pushy people."

"Oh, I know what you mean," Shawn agreed.

Felice nodded. "Auguste wanted to come to the dinner to keep an eye on his paintings—can you imagine? I told him absolutely not. I'm afraid I told him I would be hanging Joseph's newest painting here at the restaurant, so don't be surprised if he shows up to guard it. Of course, now it won't be here, since we're moving the dinner to my house, but—"

Nancy felt she should warn Felice. "Listen, Mrs. Wainwright," she said, "I'd be wary of Auguste Spaziente if I were you. He seems desperate to get that painting. If you tell your security people about him, they can make sure he's kept off the premises tomorrow night."

"What? Do you think he'd steal the painting?" Felice asked, wide-eyed.

"Or maybe he's after the ruby," Nancy said.

Felice smiled confidently. "No one is getting that ruby, my dear. My system is foolproof, and Auguste Spaziente is no one to worry about. He's just a pushy, greedy old man. But thank you for your concern."

Shawn walked Felice to her chauffeur-driven limo, parked in front of the restaurant. "That was a close one," he said when he returned. "I can't believe she almost canceled."

"You're a pretty fast talker," Nancy said.

A guilty look stole over Shawn's face. "You must think I'm a terrible liar. But I'm fighting for my life here, believe me."

"Won't having the dinner at her estate be hard to manage?" Nancy asked.

Shawn shrugged. "It's the best way I can safeguard myself against anything going wrong. I'm going to hire all the waiting staff from a temporary service. That way, if someone here is out to get me, they won't be there. Plus, if they've put a bomb in the dishwasher, or whatever, it won't affect the dinner. And I would have had to close the restaurant to regular business on a Saturday night. Now I'll be able to keep the Arizona House open and make some more money."

"Makes sense," Nancy agreed. "By the way, have you talked to Loreen lately?"

Shawn shook his head, and Nancy told him about the message from Le St. Tropez on Loreen's tape.

"I don't think Loreen would sell me out like that," Shawn said. "But I was wrong about Jack, so who knows?"

"Shawn," Nancy said quietly, "I talked to Jack. There are a few things you should know." Gently, Nancy told Shawn the accusation Jack had made against Shawn's father.

Shawn sat down heavily in his chair. "Do you know what? I'm not all that surprised. Dad always seemed to have a lot more money than Jack. As I got older, I often wondered why. I figured Jack spent all of his."

"I'm sorry," Nancy said.

"It's not exactly cheery news, but I'm not crushed. Dad and I were never close." Shawn was quiet for a moment. "Did Jack tell you why he wanted the triangles from those pictures?"

"It wasn't Jack who slashed the paintings," Nancy reminded him.

"You're saying there's a wild card in this pack," Shawn said grimly.

"There's the man who slashed the paintings and there's Auguste Spaziente. Two wild cards," Nancy said.

"Could you do me a favor, Nancy?" Shawn asked. "I'd like you to work here tomorrow."

"No problem," Nancy said.

Shawn looked relieved. "Leaving this place on a Saturday makes me very nervous, but I have to be at the Wainwright dinner. I'd feel better if you were keeping an eye on things."

"I'll be here, don't worry," Nancy said.

That evening, Nancy went up to her room early. The last few days had exhausted her. When she turned off the light, however, sleep didn't come easily. She couldn't stop mulling over the case. There was a thread here—something that tied the two Spazientes, Felice Wainwright, and the paintings together. What was it?

On Saturday morning, Nancy drove over to Le St. Tropez. She wanted to talk to Edward, the man who'd called Loreen. Perhaps she could find out how Loreen was connected to Le St. Tropez.

The parking lot was full. As Nancy was about to walk into the restaurant, she nearly bumped into Loreen, who was coming out the front door. "What are you doing here?" Loreen snapped.

"Meeting a friend for lunch," Nancy replied. "What are *you* doing?"

"None of your business," Loreen said, pushing past. Nancy watched as she got into her car and peeled out of the parking lot.

Inside the posh restaurant, Nancy asked for Edward, but was told he wasn't in. Disappointed, she headed home.

That wasn't a total waste of time, Nancy told herself as she drove. Now she had proof that Loreen was still in touch with someone at Le St. Tropez. Unfortunately, she hadn't found anything to connect Loreen with Spaziente's paintings.

As Nancy dressed for work late that afternoon, she thought about the paintings again. The landscapes were the common thread that linked all her clues together. Auguste wanted them. So did Felice, who had two of Spaziente's paintings hanging in her house at the moment. And the paintings had been slashed at the Arizona House, the scene of many mishaps.

Remembering her visit to the art class, Nancy thought about Joseph. He had dashed off the winter painting in a single morning. Nancy had a feeling that art was not his passion. After that bungled bank robbery, he'd probably be more likely to go for a prize like the Dragon's Eye Ruby.

Nancy frowned. Joseph had taken part in a bank robbery where an elaborate security system had been outsmarted. If he were out of prison, he might very well be at Felice's mansion tonight.

But Joseph was behind bars. Only his paintings made it out the prison doors. What did that mean?

Nancy arrived at the Arizona House by six. "Hi, Elliot," she greeted the nervous young cook as she punched her time card by the back door.

"Oh, Nancy," he wailed. "I'm losing my mind. Shawn has made me the new dessert chef. This is my first night, and you won't believe who is out in the dining room."

"The president of the United States," Nancy teased.

"Harold Brackett," Elliot said. "It's very generous of him to give us all these chances, but three strikes and we're out."

"Don't worry, Elliot," Nancy said absently. "Everything will be fine."

Out in the dining room, Nancy spotted Brackett sitting alone, writing on a pad. The critic waved and smiled when he saw her.

"Hello, Mr. Brackett," Nancy said, walking over to his table. "How are you?"

"Just fine," he replied. "Tell me, have you got a painting by Joseph Spaziente hanging here?"

Nancy's heart thumped. How was Brackett involved in all this? "No. Why do you ask?"

"My friend Auguste Spaziente told me I must see

125

his nephew's work while I'm in town," Brackett said.

"Oh," Nancy said, frowning. Something told her not to reveal any more information. "No. I haven't seen the painting."

Anne Marie rushed over to take Brackett's drink order, and Nancy excused herself.

"Hi, Nan," Bess greeted her as Nancy walked into the front of the restaurant. "I'm on my way down to the ladies' room. Come along and tell me what's been going on."

"Okay, but just for a second. I can't be off the floor too long." Nancy went downstairs with Bess and filled her in on the case. While Bess listened, she fussed with her French braid. "This stubborn piece of hair keeps popping up," she said, spritzing it with a small plastic pump bottle of hair spray.

A rap came on the bathroom door. "Bess, you've got coat customers," Lee called.

"Be right there," Bess said, running out the door.

Looking at the mirror ledge, Nancy saw that her friend had left her hair spray behind. Dropping it in the deep pocket of her apron, she left the bathroom.

At the top of the stairs, Nancy was met by a flustered Anne Marie. "Have you seen Harold Brackett anywhere?" she asked. When Nancy shook her head, Anne Marie explained, "I sent Lee to look in the men's room, and he's not there. When I got to the table with his drink, he was gone."

"That's strange," Nancy said. "He didn't say anything to you?"

"Nope," Anne Marie said.

Just then, Lee came in the front door. "I saw Brackett dash out the front door as I was coming upstairs from the men's room," he said. "He was in such a hurry that this piece of paper fell from his notepad. I ran after him, but he was already in his car and zooming past me when I got to the parking lot."

"May I see the note?" Nancy asked.

"Sure," Lee said, handing it to her. "It looks like he was just doodling."

"Oh, no!" Nancy studied the paper. Her eyes widened in surprise. It was high-quality bond with a slight grain running through it.

"What's wrong?" Anne Marie asked.

"Nothing," Nancy said, not wanting to alarm them.

"Well, I'd better get back to work," Anne Marie said, turning toward the dining room. "I've already lost one customer tonight."

"And I have a party of four waiting to be seated," Lee said, following Anne Marie.

Clutching the paper, Nancy leaned against the wall. The paper contained doodles, with the number four written over and over. Then a line of question marks followed. And the name "Wainwright" was scrawled across the bottom with exclamation points after it.

Nancy could hardly believe her eyes. The *i* in "Wainwright" was bent back. The *n* was sharp. It was Auguste Spaziente's handwriting.

Harold Brackett must be Auguste Spaziente in disguise!

Or was it the other way around? Or maybe both were simply disguises.

What did the number four mean? Did it have something to do with the fourth painting? Felice had told Auguste that it would be at the restaurant. He had come looking for it, disguised as Brackett!

And now he knew the painting wasn't here. He was surely on his way to the Wainwright estate.

Nancy wasn't sure what Auguste had planned. But she suspected that the paintings were a way for Joseph to get information to his partner in crime. One Spaziente was a bank robber. The other was an imposter. These men were not collectors or creators of fine art.

They were after a bigger prize—the Dragon's Eye Ruby!

12

Danger in Disguise

Nancy dropped a coin in the restaurant pay phone and punched in Felice Wainwright's phone number. She had to warn Felice that she could be in danger.

Click . . . click . . . bzzzt. A strange noise came over the line. Nancy dialed the operator and was told that Felice's line was being checked for problems.

"Bess," Nancy said, stepping over to the coatroom and scribbling a number on an Arizona House business card. "Here is Felice's number. Keep trying to call it. Tell her not to let Auguste or Brackett into her house. It's really important."

"Okay. What's wrong?" Bess asked.

"I'll tell you when I get back," Nancy said, dashing out the front door.

It was quarter to seven when Nancy pulled up the

drive of the Wainwright estate, where she was
stopped by a uniformed security guard holding a
walkie-talkie. "I'm Nancy Drew," she told the
guard. "Mrs. Wainwright knows me. I need to talk
to her."

The guard spoke into his walkie-talkie. Finally,
he waved Nancy in.

As Nancy continued up the long drive, she was
astounded at the transformation of the place. With
the help of a party rental shop, Shawn had done an
amazing job. Tiny white lights strung from poles
twinkled festively in the early evening twilight.
White tents sheltered tables lavishly spread with
food, and crystal glassware sparkled on each table.

Nancy saw Shawn, dressed in his chef's whites,
directing a small army of waiters and waitresses
he'd hired just for the occasion. He didn't notice
her, and she had no time to talk with him. She
continued driving to the house.

The butler, Conrad, answered the door. "Come
in, Ms. Drew," he said politely. "The guard informed Mrs. Wainwright that you were coming.
Please wait in the foyer. She's in the drawing room,
talking with a gentleman at the moment. She'll be
with you shortly."

"A gentleman?" Nancy asked. "What did he look
like?"

"I couldn't say, miss," Conrad answered primly
as he walked out of the foyer.

In contrast to the hustle and bustle outside, the
mansion was calm and still. As soon as Conrad was

gone, Nancy hurried to the drawing room, where she'd met Felice the other day. Nancy peered through a crack between the high, sliding doors.

Inside, Felice was talking with Harold Brackett! Felice looked like a princess in her strapless gold gown. Her blond hair was swept sleekly back and held with a gold bow. Brackett's back was to Nancy.

"I'm so glad you want to purchase both paintings," Felice said. "Shawn Morgan sent you to the right place. You can make a check out to Joseph Spaziente, and after the auction you may take the paintings."

"I'd like them right away," Brackett said, an edge in his voice.

"All I'm asking is a few more hours so that my guests can view these paintings," Felice said.

"My dear woman, I want the paintings right now," Brackett said in a low, cool voice.

Nancy heard Conrad coming back. Quietly, she slipped through the opening in the door. Felice and Brackett seemed engrossed in their conversation and didn't notice her.

"That's out of the question," Felice said.

"I'm sorry it has to be this way," Brackett replied, his voice full of menace.

This is getting scary, Nancy thought. I'm contacting security. She was about to slip back out the door when a sudden sharp cry from Felice stopped her.

Brackett had pulled a gun from his pocket! Felice's hand flew to her mouth as she stared at it in horror.

Nancy sucked in her breath. She had to do something. A small shelf near the door held antique leather-bound books. The bookends were a pair of sculpted marble parrots. Using one hand to ease the books onto their sides, Nancy slid a parrot from the shelf. It felt heavy and solid in her hand as she moved closer and closer to Brackett.

By now Felice had spotted her. For a twinkling, their eyes met, then Felice looked away. "All right," she said to Brackett. "Take the paintings. Just don't hurt me."

Nancy came up behind Brackett, barely daring to breathe. Steeling herself, she lifted the parrot high, ready to knock the man over the head.

But just as her arm swung up, Brackett sensed her presence.

Whirling around, he grabbed her arm and sent the marble parrot crashing to the ground. Reacting quickly, Nancy landed a swift kick sharply to his shins. Brackett cried out and tossed her into a row of folding chairs.

Felice made a run for the door, but Brackett was too fast. He flung her back into the room.

Brackett held the gun on Nancy and Felice as he backed to the door and slid it completely shut. Nancy hoped Conrad had heard the commotion, but she had seen him heading down the hall. He might be out of earshot.

"Are you working with Auguste Spaziente?" Felice asked.

Brackett threw back his head and laughed. "My

dear lady. I *am* Auguste Spaziente. I'm flattered that my disguise fooled you so well."

"Who are you, really?" Nancy challenged.

He bowed mockingly. "Alex Templeton, at your service."

Just then, there was a knock at the door. Templeton ducked to the side of the door and waved his gun at Felice. "Get rid of them," he said.

Felice slid the door open a crack, revealing Conrad. "I heard a clatter," he said. "Is everything all right?"

"Mr. Brackett just bumped into some chairs," Felice answered in a calm voice.

"Very good, ma'am," Conrad said. "Oh, and Ms. Drew seems to have left the foyer. Did you speak to her?"

"No, I . . . suppose she couldn't wait," Felice said. "Thank you, Conrad." She slid the door shut.

"Well done," Brackett said, still training his gun on her.

"Why do you want these paintings so badly?" Felice asked.

"It isn't the paintings he's after," Nancy told her. "It's something hidden in the paintings."

"Clever girl," Templeton said. He waved his gun at Felice. "I wouldn't need the paintings at all if you could hand over the ruby to me."

"I can't," Felice said flatly. "It is in a safe upstairs, which is surrounded by an elaborate security system. Not even I can take it out without setting off all sorts of alarms. Every member of the security police I've hired for tonight would come running. Only the head of that team knows how to disengage the system."

"He's not the only one," Templeton sneered. "Guess who designed that system?"

"You?" Felice asked incredulously.

Templeton shook his head no.

"Joseph Spaziente," Nancy said quietly.

"Bingo," Templeton said. "You *are* a bright girl."

"Joseph was the one who helped you disengage that bank security system, wasn't he?" Nancy prodded. "He's some kind of whiz at security systems."

"You've done your homework. I'm impressed," Templeton taunted. "Yes, Joe and I were on that job together. Unfortunately, he had the bad luck to get caught."

"I still don't understand," Felice said, looking pale and shaky.

"Joe knows every inch of your security system. He used to work as an engineer for a big security company, and he designed your system before turning to his life of crime. When we heard you were auctioning off the ruby—well, it was just too tempting a chance to pass up."

"But Joe is in jail," Nancy interjected.

"Right," Templeton said. "And all his mail is censored. He sent me a coded letter outlining the plan, but it would have been impossible for him to simply send me a map of the circuitry for the system. The authorities would have picked up on it in a second. And then, thanks to Mrs. Wainwright

134

and her charming little art program, Joe came up with the perfect plan."

"He drew bits of circuitry in the tree bark on the lower left-hand corner of four nearly identical paintings," Nancy said.

"Spring, summer, autumn, and winter," Templeton sang out gleefully. "He was so careful. If he mapped out the whole thing in one painting, some guard might have figured out what was going on. What Joe didn't plan on was Mrs. Wainwright becoming such a big fan of his. He didn't expect to have his work displayed in restaurants and this fancy mansion. He thought she'd just hand them over to his dear old Uncle Auguste. You've made my life very difficult, Mrs. Wainwright."

"So you tracked the first two paintings to the Arizona House and posed as the food critic Harold Brackett," Nancy said.

Templeton chortled with laughter. "I simply went to the restaurant to figure a way to get the paintings. Then that dear coat-check girl—what was her name? Oh yes! Bess—she decided that I was the famous food critic Harold Brackett. And when I heard there was trouble at the restaurant— which, you may recall, I experienced firsthand— well, everything fell into place."

"*Bess* gave you the idea to vandalize the paintings?" Nancy asked.

"I'm afraid she did. Someone was already wreaking havoc at the restaurant, anyway, so I merely joined the fun. I slashed the paintings and took the pieces I needed, figuring the real restaurant gremlin would get the blame."

Templeton paused and frowned at Nancy. "But I didn't count on *you* gumming everything up. Every time I turned around, there you were. There seemed to be no getting rid of you. First you trailed me right into a car wash. I got soaked running out of that car in the middle of the wash cycle! Then when I arrived here as Uncle Auguste, I ran into you again. And now you're *here!* What is it with you? Don't you have a prom to go to, or something?"

"It takes more than a threatening note and some Seconal in my water to scare me off," Nancy replied.

"Oh, yes, the Seconal. I wanted to keep the mishaps going at the restaurant, sort of a distraction to keep you from making the connection to the ruby. And, if it scared you a little, all the better."

"And you kept returning to the Arizona House, posing as Harold Brackett, to see if the fourth painting had turned up," Nancy surmised.

"It was a perfect cover," Templeton said cheerfully. Then his expression grew serious. "Now, Mrs. Wainwright, I need you to remove the two paintings from the wall. I hate to be ungallant, but I don't want to put my gun down."

Standing on one of the wooden chairs, Felice took the winter scene off the wall and laid it on the long cherry table. Then she climbed up on the table and removed the autumn scene. She placed it on the table next to the other painting.

"Both of you stand together, right here where I can see you," Templeton said, gesturing with the gun for Nancy to move closer to Felice.

Templeton removed a utility knife from his pocket. With quick, decisive motions, he slashed two perfect triangles from the lower left corner of each painting. Then, placing the gun on the table beside him, he reached into his pocket and produced a small bottle of turpentine and a rag. He doused the rag with the turpentine and began wiping the triangles.

"Perfect," he mumbled to himself as he examined the intricate pencil marks revealed once the paint was wiped away. "I get it. This makes sense." From inside his pocket he produced the first two triangles, which had also been wiped clean of paint.

"I saw some strange lines among Joseph Spaziente's notes," Nancy said. "Was that a map of the circuitry?"

"Give the lady a prize," Templeton said. "Joe hid a diagram beneath each of the trees. Now I know exactly how to get through the security system. The fourth quadrant, hidden under the delightful winter scene, tells me how not to trip the invisible laser alarm. It looks like the Dragon's Eye Ruby will soon belong to me."

"You really are insane," Felice said defiantly. "Do you honestly think you can walk out with the ruby right under the noses of all these people?"

"I've done it before," Templeton replied. "And I

am about to do it again." He pointed with his gun toward a door at the far corner of the room. "Right now I'll be stashing you ladies in the old servants' quarters."

"I don't have servants' quarters," Felice bluffed.

"Call them what you will, but I know you have a boarded-up section at the back of the house. I saw it when I was here surveying the property last week."

"What?" Felice asked, looking both surprised and confused.

"I'm sure you recall the night your alarm was tripped. I never start a job without first getting to know every inch of the place I plan to rob. Unfortunately, I didn't have all the information I needed, and I tripped the alarm. I spent hours flattened in a shadow against your roof, waiting for the security guards to leave. What a dismal night that was. In any case, I found the perfect place to stash you two. Now please, start walking toward the door."

At gunpoint, Nancy and Felice walked through the door and up a narrow flight of stairs. Knowing they'd soon be trapped in some boarded-up room, Nancy decided it was time to make a move.

"Oooph!" she cried out, pretending to stumble on the narrow stairway.

"Get up," Templeton snapped.

Felice was ahead of her on the stairs. "Are you all right?" she asked.

"I think I twisted my ankle," Nancy moaned.

As Templeton bent forward to check her foot, Nancy kicked him hard in the stomach. He grunted, but caught his balance against the wall. Nancy lunged for his gun. For a moment she thought she had it safely in her grasp. Then, with his left hand, Templeton grabbed her hand in an iron grip.

The next thing Nancy knew, she and Templeton were tumbling down the stairs, both their hands still wrapped around the gun!

13

The Dragon's Eye Ruby

When they hit the first landing, Templeton fell hard on top of Nancy, knocking the breath out of her. He yanked the gun from her hand and staggered to his feet.

"Playtime is over, ladies," Templeton said angrily as Nancy pulled herself to her feet. "Now, up those stairs!"

Bruised and discouraged, Nancy climbed the four flights behind Felice. Finally they entered a dark, narrow corridor with sloped ceilings.

"Inside," Templeton told them, pushing open the door leading to a small room with boarded-over windows. Nancy saw that the room was empty except for a freestanding pine wardrobe.

Templeton's eyes danced maliciously as he pulled a pair of surgical gloves from his pocket and wriggled into them. "I wouldn't want to leave any messy prints on your vault," he said, laughing.

"Look what I found during my little exploration of your home," Templeton added, holding up a skeleton key. "Thanks for leaving this on a hook for me. It locks every door on this hall." With that, Templeton shut the door and locked it.

"I certainly was a fool," Felice said darkly. "There I was, thinking I was promoting the career of a great, new artistic talent."

"Don't blame yourself," Nancy said. "Right now we have to concentrate on getting out of here." She pulled on the boards over the single window, but they wouldn't budge. "Can you think of anything?" she asked Felice.

Felice shook her head. "At least he didn't hurt us. Don't you think that's strange, considering that we know what he looks like and we can connect him to Joseph Spaziente?"

"It's very strange," Nancy said grimly. "He's probably coming back—which is why we have to get out of here." She rattled the door and studied the lock. Too bad she hadn't brought along her lock-picking kit when she'd dressed for work. "You don't have a hairpin, do you?" she asked Felice.

"I'm afraid not," Felice told her.

Nancy slammed her hand on the door in frustration. "There's got to be a way out!"

Felice's face brightened. "I'm not sure it's a way out, but . . ."

"But what?" Nancy prodded.

"Help me move this wardrobe," Felice said.

141

Together the two of them pushed the heavy piece of furniture. "There," Felice said. Behind the wardrobe was a small cabinet built into the wall, its door held with a wooden latch.

"What is it?" Nancy asked.

"It's a dumbwaiter," Felice told her. "Way back when this house was built, the servants did live up here. The dumbwaiter leads straight down to the kitchen. There is an opening at every floor. It was used to deliver meals and whatnot to the various floors. It saved the staff from having to constantly run up and down the stairs."

Felice unlatched the door, and she and Nancy looked down the dark, narrow shaft. "Oh, dear!" Felice sighed. "The dumbwaiter box and the pulleys have been removed. I had hoped we could lower ourselves in the dumbwaiter. It was like a mini elevator."

"But it's wide enough for me to climb down," Nancy said. "Give me a boost."

"No!" Felice gasped. "It's a four-story drop. If you slip, you'll be killed."

"I'll hold on tight," Nancy insisted. "It's our only chance."

"You won't be able to get in on the third floor," Felice told her. "A bookshelf has been built over the dumbwaiter opening there."

"Then I'll go down to the second floor," Nancy said.

Felice nodded. "That will open to my bedroom. There's only a watercolor painting over that opening. A good push should be enough to open the door . . . I hope."

Summoning all her courage, Nancy climbed into the shaft. Slats of thin wood gave her something to clutch. The shaft was narrow enough so that Nancy could brace her back against one wall with her feet pressed against the opposite wall.

"Be careful when you come out into my bedroom," Felice added. "The room with the vault is right next door. Templeton may hear you."

"I'll watch out for him," Nancy promised.

Moving inch by inch, Nancy slid along the shaftway. Every muscle in her body was tight with tension. By the time she reached the third floor, she was engulfed in darkness.

Nancy kept descending. After what seemed an eternity, she came to the second floor opening.

Stopping just above the door, she kicked it hard with the bottom of one foot. The kick threw her off balance, and she had to save herself by grabbing a slat of rickety wood. "One more time," she told herself. *Bam!* She hit the door with all her might. There was a dull thud, and she knew the painting had fallen to the ground. With a creak, the dumbwaiter door fell slightly open.

Nancy clutched the wooden frame of the opening and swung her legs through into Felice's bedroom, listening for Templeton.

Inside the house, everything was quiet. The lights and sounds of the party filtered through Felice's lace curtains.

Soundlessly, Nancy dropped to the thick white carpet. She stole to the open bedroom door and cautiously peeked out, then ducked back. Templeton was just slipping out of the next room. And in his gloved hand was a purple velvet bag.

He had the ruby!

Nancy waited for a moment, then looked again. Templeton was heading down the stairs at the far end of the hall. It would be much too dangerous to confront him now. But she could follow him out and get help from the security force.

As she passed the room with the safe, Nancy noticed an unconscious guard on the floor beside the open safe. She would send help for him as soon as she could.

As Nancy ran for the main stairs, a smoky smell hit her nose. Then she saw smoke billowing from under a door. The door probably opened onto the narrow stairs they'd taken to the servants' quarters.

So that was Templeton's plan for them! He was going to burn the house down, starting with the upper quarters. Even if the fire department was able to save the bottom of the house, the servants' wing would be destroyed—along with Felice.

Nancy pulled on the door. It was locked. Now she could no longer hold back. She had to get downstairs to alert someone. Felice's life depended on it.

Nancy looked down the stairs. Templeton was gone. Let him go, Nancy thought. Felice's life was more important than the ruby. She bounded down the stairs to call the fire department.

144

Suddenly a strong hand sheathed in rubber reached out and clapped her mouth shut.

"You don't give up, do you?" Templeton growled. Another gloved hand tightened around her throat.

At that instant Nancy remembered the can of Bess's hairspray she'd stuck in her pocket. Desperately, she grabbed it and squirted in the direction of Templeton's face.

"Aaah!" he cried, loosening his grip. He balled up his fists and rubbed his eyes.

Gasping, Nancy pulled away from him. In a flash she saw that he'd set the velvet bag down on the flat bottom part of the banister. Nancy darted her hand out, snapped up the bag, and ran like mad.

She was racing down the hall when Conrad stepped out of a doorway. "Call the fire department!" Nancy shouted. "Felice is trapped upstairs in the old servants' quarters. And the guard by the safe has been hurt."

The butler paused, confuse. He was quickly shoved aside by Templeton, who tore down the hall in hot pursuit of the ruby.

Nancy ran out into the night air. A small orchestra played classical music as lavishly dressed guests chatted, champagne glasses in hand.

The guests seemed barely aware of her as Nancy ran out onto an open expanse of lawn. This is crazy, she thought. She was surrounded by people, yet no one would help her. Templeton was quickly overtaking her. "Help!" she cried.

Suddenly Templeton hit her with a flying tackle,

sending her crashing to the ground. Wrenching her wrist, he yanked the velvet bag from her hand.

Nancy rolled on the damp grass and grabbed his ankle. Templeton went down with a thud.

Then Nancy looked up and saw six security guards encircling them, revolvers drawn and aimed. In the distance, she heard the shrill scream of approaching fire trucks.

For a moment Nancy stared into the barrel of one of the guard's revolvers. She swallowed hard. Surely the security guards didn't think she had attempted to steal the ruby.

Nancy was relieved when she saw Felice hurry up to the guards. The woman was disheveled and soot-covered. Beside her was the head officer. "Let Nancy up," she told them. "That man is the thief."

One guard reached down and helped Nancy to her feet. Nancy brushed off her pants, then bent and picked up the velvet bag that lay on the grass. "Here," she said, handing it to Felice. "I believe this belongs to you."

Felice took the crimson stone from the bag. The size of a golf ball, the ruby shone in the twinkling white lights as though it contained some sort of magic. "Yes, it's mine," Felice agreed. "And I can't wait until it belongs to someone else."

The next afternoon, Nancy drove to the Arizona House. She arrived as the staff was serving Sunday brunch.

"Look at this," Bess said, running to greet her.

She held up the front page of the morning newspaper. " 'International Jewel Thief Thwarted by Local Heroine!' " Bess read the headline. "It says here that Alex Templeton is wanted in three countries for similar jewel thefts," she added. "He's a master of disguise, too. He even posed as a policeman once to rob a jewelry store."

Nancy took the paper from her and skimmed it. The article described how Conrad had saved Felice Wainwright by braving the smoke to unlock the doors that had her trapped upstairs. But mostly it featured an interview with Felice, in which she recounted how Nancy had caught Templeton.

The party had been disrupted, but the auction had been held, anyway. The ruby was sold for over a million dollars, all of which Felice was donating to build a new wing at the hospital in downtown River Heights.

"I didn't realize what I was getting you into, Nancy," Shawn said, coming into the hallway from the dining room. "I hope you won't hold it against me." He looked earnestly at her.

"Not at all," Nancy answered. "It was very interesting. And Loreen turned out to be completely innocent, except for tripping me. All she's guilty of is being crazy about you."

Just then, Loreen came rushing in the front door. "Shawn, I have to speak to you!"

"What is it?" Shawn asked.

"It's Harold Brackett," she replied, tossing her red hair over her shoulder. "I was just over at Le St.

Tropez, talking to Edward, the manager, about a job. Brackett was eating lunch there. They'd convinced him to give them a second chance, I guess. Anyway, we had the wrong guy. The real Harold Brackett is an older man, not—"

"We know," Shawn broke in, smiling.

"You do?" Loreen asked.

"Yep, we do," Bess told her sheepishly.

"Well, the real Harold Brackett is on his way here for dessert," Loreen continued breathlessly. "I heard him talking on the phone to his editor in Chicago."

"Why are you telling me this?" Shawn asked.

"Because I've been a real jerk. I'm sorry for the way I acted. I've been a green-eyed monster." Loreen turned to Nancy. "And I'm really sorry about tripping you. I don't know what came over me."

"I accept your apology," Nancy said.

Shawn looked at Loreen. "Why don't we talk about this over supper tonight?" he asked. "We have a lot to discuss."

"I'd like that," Loreen said softly.

"Oh, I knew it! I knew you two lovebirds would get back together," cheered Elliot, who was passing by at that moment.

"Elliot!" Shawn exclaimed. "You'd better get back in that kitchen. The real Harold Brackett is coming for dessert."

Elliot jerked his thumb toward the lounge, where Jack was sitting at the bar. "There's a *real* dessert chef in there," he said. "He wants to talk to you, Shawn, but he's very nervous."

"Excuse me just a moment," Shawn said, going into the lounge.

Nancy returned her uniform to Loreen and said goodbye to everyone. She was on her way out when Shawn and Jack appeared in the hallway.

"Meet my new partner," Shawn said. "Jack came here to apologize to me, but I figure I also owe something to him. I can't undo what my father did, but I can sell Jack a partnership at a very reasonable price."

"That's great," Nancy said.

"Now let me get into the kitchen and prepare for this critic," Jack said. For once, he didn't look so grumpy.

"It looks like a new beginning for the Arizona House," Nancy said, a broad smile on her face.

"It sure does," Shawn agreed. "Thanks to you, Nancy Drew."